MORE
Laughter in
Appalachia
SOUTHERN MOUNTAIN HUMOR

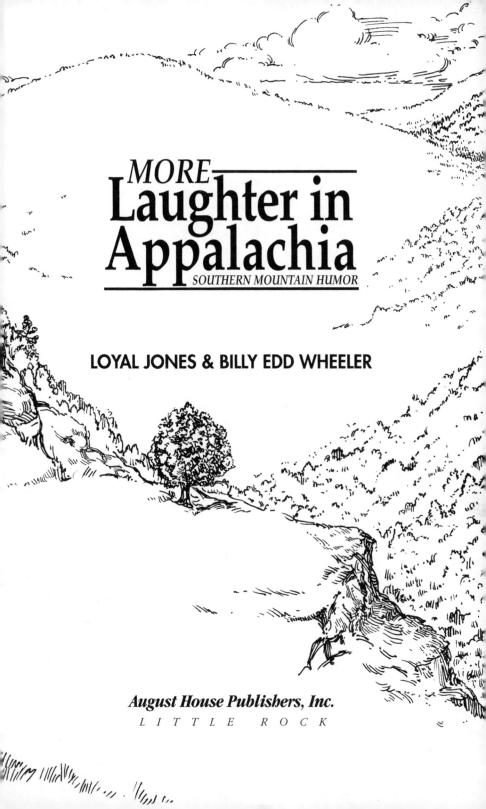

MORE Laughter in Appalachia

SOUTHERN MOUNTAIN HUMOR

LOYAL JONES & BILLY EDD WHEELER

August House Publishers, Inc.

LITTLE ROCK

Published 1995 by August House, Inc.,
P.O. Box 3223, Little Rock, Arkansas, 72203,
501-372-5450.

Printed in the United States of America

10 9 8 7 6 5 4 3 2 1 PB

LIBRARY OF CONGRESS CATALOGING-IN-PUBLICATION DATA
More Laughter in Appalachia /
[compiled by] Loyal Jones and Billy Edd Wheeler.
p.   cm.
ISBN 0-87483-411-2 (pbk.) : $10.95
1. Mountain whites (Southern States)—Humor
2. American wit and humor—Appalachian Region.
3. Appalachian Region—Social life and customs—Humor.
I. Jones, Loyal, 1928- . II. Wheeler, Billy Edd.
PN6231.A65M67   1995
818'.540208974—dc20   94-40905

Executive editor: Liz Parkhurst
Project editor: Rufus Griscom
Design director: Ted Parkhurst
Cover art and design: Wendell E. Hall

The paper used in this publication meets the minimum requirements of
the American National Standard for Information Sciences—Permanence of
Paper for Printed Library Materials, ANSI Z39.48-1984.

AUGUST HOUSE, INC.   PUBLISHERS   LITTLE ROCK

For all of you who know—
or need to find out—
that humor is the best cushion on our
sometimes bumpy road of life.

Also from Loyal Jones, Billy Edd Wheeler,
and August House:

Hometown Humor U.S.A. (Jones and Wheeler), 1991

Curing the Cross-Eyed Mule (Jones and Wheeler), 1989

The Preacher Joke Book (Jones), 1989

Outhouse Humor (Wheeler), 1988

Laughter in Appalachia (Jones and Wheeler), 1987

Contents

Acknowledgments

We are grateful to all of our friends who have shared humor with us. First, we appreciate all those who came to the Fourth Festival of Appalachian Humor at Berea College in July of 1993. We especially thank Dr. Jim W. Miller, Professor of German Language and Literature at Western Kentucky University, and Dr. Howard R. Pollio, Professor of Psychology and Senior Research Fellow at the University of Tennessee, for their insightful presentations which are included in this book. We also thank the invited humorists who kept us in stitches: Judge Ray Corns of Frankfort, Kentucky; Sam Venable of Knoxville, Tennessee; Virginia Kilgore of Nashville, Tennessee; George Daugherty of Elkview, West Virginia; and Marc and Anita Pruett of Asheville, North Carolina. We also thank those who came to the festival to enjoy the humor and who shared material with us that is included in this book.

In addition, we thank our many friends who are always telling us stories—on the street, in the supermarket, in all kinds of places. We've had wonderful letters from people who say our humor has lightened their load in daily coping: in the hospital, in the nursing home, and one fellow in prison! When such people write they often send their favorite stories, or their long-departed father's or mother's favorites. When we speak at gatherings, we often have people waiting to tell us their best one. Usually, we have time to make a note or two so as to remember it. We really appreciate you. Specifically we want to thank the following for their material: Dr. Thomas D. Clark, Lexington, Kentucky; Col. Ed Ward, Bledsoe, Kentucky; John Ed McConnell, Frankfort, Kentucky; Howard White, Greenbrier, Tennessee; Bonnie Collins, West Union, West Virginia; Dr. Kenneth and Jewell Israel, Candler, North Carolina; the Rev. J. Harold Stephens, Shelbyville, Tennessee; Paul Graham, Benham, Kentucky; and Chet Atkins, C.G.P., Nashville, Tennessee.

Finally, we want to thank the children in the P.I.G.S. (Perfectly Ingenious Group of Students) of White Hall Elementary School, Madison County, Kentucky, who are learning verbal skills by collecting, telling, and writing stories, a great example of Kentucky's effort to reform education. When one of us was invited to tell tales at their school, they presented him with a book of jokes, tales, stories, riddles and the like that they had collected from family and neighbors. Some of this material is included. Thank you, Chelsea, Jara, Mary, Cie, Julie, both Tylers, and your creative teachers.

And we sheepishly thank those whose stories are included but whose names have been forgotten. We're not as young as we used to be, and sometimes our memories slip. There are four advantages to that, you know:

1. Everybody you meet is a new friend.
2. Every joke you hear is as good as new.
3. You can hide your own Easter eggs.
4. We forget what this one is.

Billy Edd Wheeler
Swannanoa, North Carolina

Loyal Jones
Berea, Kentucky

INTRODUCTION:

Heaven High and Hell Deep

We believe that the humor we have collected for this book is entertaining, but we believe it is also serious in that it is rooted in our culture. We want to provide some insight into that elusive element we call humor as well as reflect something about this place called Appalachia. We think Appalachian people are distinctive, and the humor we circulate reveals something important about us. In this book we looked for jokes and stories that are Appalachian, or at least related to this region. We are well aware, however, that much included here can also be found in some form elsewhere, since our lives are similar to those of people in other places. Thus the same kind of joke may serve them as well as us.

A good example of this occurred when a group of Tibetan exiles visited Berea College to ask that some of their young people be admitted. They were among those who had moved with the Dalai Lama to India when the Chinese took over their country. After talking seriously with them about preserving culture in exile and other such topics, we asked them for a Tibetan joke. All heads turned to their recognized storyteller who astonishingly told a variant of a story well-known in Appalachia, which went something like this:

Two Tibetan exiles in India decided to go back to Tibet and visit relatives. They went in an old flat-bed truck, had a nice visit, and headed back home. Not being too friendly toward the Chinese oppressors, they decided they ought not to go home empty-handed. So when they went by a hog farm they got out and caught a big hog. Since they had no enclosure on the truck, they simply put it on the seat between them, and drove on.

One of them thought about their deed, though, and said, "You know, when we get to the border, there's going to be a guardhouse there with soldiers, and they're going to see this hog and arrest us. We'll be in trouble."

About that time, however, they went by an army barracks, and saw an officer's uniform swinging on a clothesline. One of them jumped out and took that uniform and put it on the hog. He looked good with gold braid and red trim, hat and all.

Sure enough, they got to the border and there was a guardhouse. Soldiers came out, peered into the cab, saw the officer insignia, came to attention, saluted, and waved them by.

Then one of the soldiers said to the others, "You know, I've seen some ugly officers in my time, but d_____d if that one didn't looked like a hog!"

In the mountains that joke is usually about the Johnson boys who steal a hog and are stopped by the sheriff. His comment is, "I've been the sheriff here twenty years, and I've seen a lot of ugly people, but d_____d if that Oink Johnson ain't the ugliest S.O.B. I ever seen!"

That joke, like others, comments on the relationship between people of little power and prestige dealing with those who have it, or those who perceive themselves to be superior in some way or other. Here in the mountains we have had lots of people we'll collectively call missionaries, who have come to the mountains troubled about our being different from them, and thinking they are way better than we are. They assume they are in a position to make us just like them, and that we want to be just like them. There is a cycle of stories mountain people love that turns the tables on such people. Here's one version:

A missionary goes up to a mountain woman in the door of a modest home and asks, "Do you know that Jesus died for your sins?"

She says, "Well, you know, I live so far back up the holler that I don't hardly ever get any news, and I hadn't even heard that he was sick."

The missionary says, "I see you are living in darkness."

She says, "Yes, I've been trying to get John to cut me a window on the south side of the house to get more light."

He tries another tack, "Who's John?"

"Why, he's my husband."

"Where is he?"

"Off hunting."

"What, off hunting on the Sabbath, when the Judgment Day is coming?"

"When is it?"

"Why, it might be next month or it might be next week."

"Well, when you find out, let me know. John will want to go both days."

The attraction of this joke is that the woman perceived to be ignorant is making a fool of the one who feels superior. We take delight in stories that allow us to win. The Tibetan joke serves the same purpose. Two defenseless Tibetans outwit the Chinese army.

The first problem in collecting Appalachian humor (or crafts or music or whatever) is that it is not clear where Appalachia begins and ends. What are its boundaries? Do all who live here—

both well-to-do and the poor—think of themselves as Appalachians? Is it more a state of mind or an actual place? There has been much debate on these questions. Perhaps a philosophical or literary definition is better than a geographical one. James Still, the Knott County, Kentucky, writer thought about it some, and came up with an eloquent and personal answer:

> Appalachia is that somewhat mythical region with no known borders. If such an area exists in terms of geography, such a domain as has shaped the lives and endeavors of men and women from pioneer days to the present and given them an independence and an outlook and a vision such as is often attributed to them, I trust to be understood for imagining the heart of it to be in the hills of Eastern Kentucky where I have lived and feel at home and where I have exercised as much freedom and peace as the world allows. (James Still, *The Wolfpen Notebooks*. Lexington: University Press of Kentucky, 1991.)

Now that's the kind of writing only a day and night, full-time, forever-thinking-forever-writing writer comes up with. But as much as we like that statement, it was James Still's many quotes (in *The Wolfpen Notebooks*) collected from his Knott County neighbors that really knocked us down, gave us the idea for this essay (and one of us the idea for a song!): *"This is my farm, every acre of it. I own it heaven high and hell deep."*

Some will take exception to the word *own* and think the man who said it could just as well have said, I *love* it heaven high and hell deep," and he probably did mean that too. It's the kind of passion and pride and colorful language Appalachians use when talking about their homeplaces.

These passages do suggest that land and place are central to the sense of being Appalachian. It was the land that caused the first settlers (from England, Wales, Scotland-by-way-of-Ireland,

and Germany) to come here. They wanted to be free of those powers that had oppressed them and to exercise the kind of freedom that James Still celebrates. They brought with them treasures of memory: old world folktales, tragic ballads, love songs, fiddle tunes for dancing, riddles, humorous stories, songs and rhymes, and of course a commitment to a personal kind of religion out of a radical tradition. They were mostly Calvinists in the early days, and thus they had a strong sense of human fallibility. They saw humor in attempts to appear to be better than they were capable of being. They knew their share of hardship, and they compensated, or coped, by having a humorous outlook. Sickness and death came early, and knowing they could not prevail against these certainties, they chose to keep a modicum of dignity by laughing at the inevitable.

In addition to dangers and hardship, they had to deal with those who came from afar with some sort of program in mind—to relieve them of their timber and minerals, to win their souls, to improve their minds, to enlist them in all sorts of projects. They learned to cope with all of this the best they could, their last-ditch stand being humor. And humor was also useful for entertaining themselves in dull moments.

There is a lot of it, and we are glad to pull some of it together here, in yet another collection. After four humor festivals and three books, we think we've become pretty well acquainted with Appalachian humor and we marvel that new stuff keeps coming. Almost all herein is new, although we have included variants of stories that have appeared in earlier books and have repeated just a few choice items.

Howard Pollio and Jim Miller's essays at the end of the book have helped a lot in defining humor. Pollio gives some great insights into the themes in humor and on how a laugh helps us to throw off for a moment oppressive societal pressures, while Miller centers on Appalachian humor in particular. Miller cites the Appalachian writer Wilma Dykeman who said that the Appalachian experience is "as unique as churning butter and as universal as getting born." Appalachian humor truly is both here and everywhere, particular and universal.

We can't imagine someone living in New York City, or Miami, or any big city anywhere saying, "I love this place heaven high and hell deep." That is not to say we think our humor is better or funnier than metropolitan humor. It is from the same wellspring of what makes people laugh the world over. We just think ours has a special taste, and it satisfies in bits and pieces but creates a hunger that brings you back for more. It is perhaps uniquely colorful because it is home-grown and springs up in a "somewhat mythical region with no known borders." Our Appalachia is a place we feel passionate about, a place we love— heaven high and hell deep!

Come. Have a taste.

Billy Edd Wheeler
Swannanoa, North Carolina

Loyal Jones
Berea, Kentucky

RURAL LIFE:

Pig Tales, Sheep Yarns, and other Farm Fables

Truckin' Along

A man from the southern mountains had to go to California. It was his first trip by airplane and the flight made four or five scheduled stops on the way. The man watched the gas truck refueling the plane at each stop with great interest. When they landed at their destination, his seatmate commented, "We made pretty good time in spite of the stops."

The mountaineer replied, "Yes, and that feller with the gas truck did all right too."

The late Dr. Raymond B. Drukker
BEREA, KENTUCKY

Good Match

A lot of mergers have been going on lately. The best one I've heard about is when the local veterinarian and the taxidermist went into business together. They hung out a sign: EITHER WAY, YOU'LL GET YOUR DOG BACK.

Loyal Jones

Better Footing

A country fellow was going to town to see his first train, and he decided to walk on the railroad tracks. The train came up

behind him, and he took off down the track as fast as he could, just staying ahead of the locomotive. He ran all the way to town, where the train slowed and stopped. The depot agent who had watched him approach asked, "Why didn't you just get off the tracks?" The fellow gasped, "I knowed if I got off in that plowed ground, he'd catch me for sure."

Loyal Jones

Cow Accessories

The local car dealer, who was known to have taken advantage of several people in the community, informed a farmer that he was coming over to purchase a cow. The farmer priced the cow as follows:

BASIC COW: $499.95
Shipping and handling: $35.75
Extra stomach: $79.25
Two-tone exterior: $142.10
Produce storage compartment: $126.50
Heavy-duty straw chopper: $189.60
Automatic fly swatter: $88.50
Four-spigot high output drain system: $149.20
Genuine cowhide upholstery: $179.90
Deluxe dual horns: $59.25
Automatic fertilizer attachment: $339.40
4-by-4 traction drive assembly: $884.16
Pre-delivery wash and comb: $69.80
FARMER'S SUGGESTED LIST PRICE: $2,843.36
Additional dealer adjustments: $300.00
TOTAL LIST PRICE (including options): $3,143.36

Howard White
GREENBRIER, TENNESSEE

Marketable Mule

This farmer had this mule he used to do chores around the farm. One time the mule got hemmed up in the barn and they had three or four people in there trying to catch him. The farmer's mother-in-law got in the way, and the mule kicked her to death.

Well, it was a sad occasion, and at the funeral they had all kinds of people come, hundreds of them. The family thought it was wonderful that the lady had so many friends.

Come to find out, most of these people had come there trying to buy that mule!

Marc Pruett
ASHEVILLE, NORTH CAROLINA

Freezing Hot

That same old mule passed away a year or two after that. What happened was the farmer had that mule out plowing a piece of ground next to a big field of popcorn, and it got so hot the popcorn started popping and so deep the old mule saw all that white stuff and thought it was snow, and laid down and froze to death!

Marc Pruett

Optimist

There was this young boy who was always an optimist. He came upon a huge pile of horse dung, ran and got a shovel and started digging.

"The dung is piled so high," the boy cried, "I know there must be a pony in here somewhere."

William J. Usury
WASHINGTON D.C.

Savvy City Cyclist

A New York stock broker decided to see America, so he took

off on a bicycle and eventually found himself pedaling through some lovely West Virginia hill country. He stopped as often as possible to ask for a drink of water or ask for directions, and thus was able to engage people in conversation. He found West Virginians to be quite friendly and hospitable.

One day he thought he would check out how smart they were, so he playfully asked a sheep farmer near Buckhannon, "Sir, if I guess how many sheep you have on that hillside there, would you give me one of them?"

"Shucks, yeah," the farmer replied.

The man looked closely at the large flock for a minute or two, then said, "I think you've got 347 sheep up there."

The farmer was amazed and said, "By golly, that's right. Go ahead and pick up your animal," which the New Yorker did.

As he was walking away the farmer asked him, "Say mister, if I guess what you do for a living, would you give my animal back?"

The man agreed. The farmer said, "You're a New York stock broker."

It was time for the New Yorker to be amazed. He said, "That's right. How in the world did you guess?"

"That's my dog you just picked up," the farmer said smiling.

Bruce McBrackney
BEAUFORT, SOUTH CAROLINA

Progressive Hog Farming

A pig farmer in eastern Kentucky had some old sweet apple trees and sometimes he would hold his pet pig up and let him eat apples off the tree.

One day the County Agent, who had just graduated from Berea College and knew a lot about hog nutrition, came by while the farmer was doing this. He said, "Mister, what in the world are you doing?"

"I'm feeding my pig," the man responded.

The agent said, "You know there's better ways of doing that, don't you? You could buy a mix like Purina that would be better balanced, be a lot healthier, and—"

"What would be the advantage of doing that?" the farmer asked.

"For one thing," the agent said, "you could feed him and grow him faster. You could save a lot of time."

The farmer said, "What's time to a hog?"

The late Dr. Francis S. Hutchins
BEREA, KENTUCKY

Whinney-Hop Burgers

A man opened up a drive-in restaurant and advertised rabbit burgers. The food and drug people came to inspect and found he was mixing in horse meat. They said that in order for him to call them rabbit burgers, he would have to do a fifty-fifty mix. He promised to follow instructions, and he did—one rabbit to one horse.

Roy Tincher
ADDRESS UNKNOWN

Year-Round Entertainment

A summer visitor from Florida to the Great Smokies met a mountain man, and he asked, "Whatever do you people do here in winter?"

The mountaineer replied, "Oh, we talk and laugh about the summer people."

Loyal Jones

Common Sense

The county road ran in front of my grandfather's house, which was at the bottom of a long hill. There were several other houses before you reached the top of the hill. One day a man stopped by and asked my grandfather where a certain man lived.

"Well, he lives in the last house before you get to the top of the hill."

The man asked, "How will I know which is the last house before the top of the hill?"

Grandpa thought a minute and said, "Just drive up to the top of the hill, turn around, and come back. The first house you come to will be where he lives."

Juanita Slater
WEST VIRGINIA

Ample Resources

A Russian, a Cuban, a hillbilly, and a social worker were on a train. The Russian opened a bottle of vodka, took a drink, and threw the bottle out of the window.

The hillbilly was astonished and said, "How could you do that?"

"We have much vodka in Russia. It is nothing," said the Russian.

The Cuban lit up a Havana cigar, took a puff, and threw it out the window.

The hillbilly said, "How could you do that?"

The Cuban said, "De Nada. We have much cigars in Cuba."

Thereupon, the hillbilly threw the social worker out of the window.

Stephen Spurlock
HAZARD, KENTUCKY

Showy

An uplifted Tennessean came back home for a visit from New York City where he was living. He was telling his country cousin what a wonderful place New York was. "Why, we've got one sign up there on Times Square that has a hundred thousand lights on it."

His cousin thought that information over and said, "Isn't it kind of conspicuous?"

Loyal Jones

Hillbillies Abroad

These two Tennessee boys were in New York, and they said, "Let's don't let these New Yorkers know we're from Tennessee. Let's talk real proper."

They went into a store and one said, "I'd like a pound of po-tat-oes, please." The other boy said, "Yes, and make that another pound of to-mat-oes."

The man said to them, "You guys are from Tennessee, aren't you?"

They said, "How'd you know that?"

He said, "Well, this is a hardware store!"

Chinquapin Jones
GRAVEL SWITCH, KENTUCKY

Written All over Him

There was this college student named Joe from Sand Gap, Kentucky, going to the university and majoring in business. He did very well all four years in his courses, and he got the notion that he would like to work for one of the big New York advertising firms. His professors encouraged him, and he applied and was promptly accepted. Then he got cold feet, said he wouldn't know how to act up there and was afraid he couldn't adapt. His roommate told him about a student from New York City and suggested he talk to him. So he went to see the New Yorker.

Joe told him his fears, said he was afraid people would laugh at his accent. The New Yorker said that there were all kinds of accents in New York and no one would think his stranger than the others.

He said he wouldn't know how to dress, but the fellow said that people dressed all sorts of ways in New York, cowboy out-fits, shorts, hippy clothes, three-piece suits, all sorts of things.

Then he said he was worried about food and going into restaurants, that he would feel out of place. The New Yorker said, "Look, you've got a point there, but I'll tell you what to do.

You won't be there but a day or so when your co-workers will say, 'Let's go out to lunch. Where would you like to go?' You say, 'Let's go to a Jewish delicatessen.' So, you'll go there and be seated, and a snotty waiter will come with a menu with 150 items on it. Pay no attention to it. The waiter will come back and say, 'Whadaya want?' Say, 'Bring me corned beef, thinly sliced.' He'll say, 'Whadaya want it on?' You say, 'Thin rye.' He'll say 'Whadaya want on it?' You say, 'Dijon mustard.' You'll do just fine."

So the fellow graduated, went to New York, went to work for the big company, and sure enough, in a day or two somebody said, "Let's go to lunch. Where would you like to go, and he said, "Let's go to a Jewish delicatessen."

So they went and were seated. A snotty waiter came by and threw down the menu with 150 items on it. The Kentuckian ignored it. After a while the waiter came back and said to Joe, "Whadaya want?" Joe said, "Corned beef, thinly sliced." The waiter said, "Whadaya want it on?" and Joe said, "Thin rye." But when the waiter asked, "Whadaya want on it?" Joe got rattled and said, "Mayonnaise."

The waiter stared at him for a moment, and said, "You must be from some place like Sand Gap, Kentucky."

Dr. Jeff Titon
PROVIDENCE, RHODE ISLAND

Direction Makes a Difference

There was a fellow named Sam Watson who pumped gas down in Summer Shade, Kentucky. One day a fellow drove by, stopped and asked,

"How far is it to Glasgow?"

Sam said, "24, 986 miles."

The traveller said, "I don't mean Glasgow, Scotland. I mean Glasgow, Kentucky. How far is it?"

"It's 24,986 the direction you're going, but if you turn around and head the other direction, it's eleven miles."

Col. Jim Morgan
BEREA, KENTUCKY

Strange Bedfellows

Two drunks checked into a hotel and were given a room with two double beds. They got undressed, turned off the light and both got in the same bed. One of them said, "Are you all right?"

The other one said, "No, there's somebody in bed with me."

The first one rolled over and said, "There's somebody in bed with me too."

Then he said, "Let's count to three and throw them out!"

So they counted to three, there was a great commotion, and one of them hit the floor.

The one in bed said, "Are you all right?"

The other one said, "No, he threw me out."

The one in bed said, "That's all right. Get up here with me."

The late Archie Campbell
NASHVILLE, TENNESSEE

A Tight Fit

Back in the 1920s in Winchester, Kentucky, there was a tailor's shop, and next to it there was a shoemaker's shop. The tailor and shoemaker were friendly at times, but at other times they weren't, and sometimes they had some pretty hard arguments. During one of the periods when they were not on very good terms, the tailor had a journeyman who got drunk pretty regularly, and one day he had a drunken fit and fell out the door. Some people rushed over to pick him up, and the shoemaker said, "For heaven's sake, let the man alone. That is the first fit that ever came out of that shop."

The Honorable John E. Garner
WINCHESTER, KENTUCKY

Not Even Narrow

A mountaineer was sitting on his front porch with a good view of a washed-out bridge, when a northern tourist plunged into the creek. He went down and inquired, "Didn't you see the sign?"

"Yes, I did," said the indignant tourist. It said "Narrow Bridge."

"No, no," said the mountaineer. "It said Nary a Bridge."

Jack Marema
BEREA, KENTUCKY

Turbo Bus

This man went into the bus station at Winston-Salem and asked for a ticket to Hillsville, Virginia. There is a time change between these two places that he didn't know about.

"What time does the bus leave?" he asked.

"Twelve o'clock."

"When does it get to Hillsville?"

"Twelve o'clock."

He thought about that for a moment, and the agent asked if he wanted a ticket.

"No," he said, "I just want to go down there and watch that bus take off!"

Anne Phillips
PINNACLE, NORTH CAROLINA

Flavored Flies

A county home demonstration agent visited a farm family, and they had a lot of flies. She said, "What you ought to do is get screens for your windows and put lime down in your outhouse."

The farmer studied on it and said, "Well, I'll put lime in the outhouse, but I can't afford the screens."

The next time she visited he had screens on his windows, so she asked what made him change his mind.

The farmer said, "Well, when I saw those white flies walking around on my dinner, I bought screens."

Loyal Jones

Country Fellow

People are always talking about going to the country these days. I have an old uncle who lives out in the hills of Kentucky. I went out there to see him. I drove my car on the blacktop as far as it went, then took a graveled road and then a dirt road. I had to hire a mule and wagon, and when the road ran out, I unhitched the mule and rode it for a while. Finally I had to swing across the creek on a grapevine to get to my uncle's house, and when I got there I found a note on the door that said, "Gone to the country for the weekend."

Louis "Grandpa" Jones
RIDGETOP, TENNESSEE

I'll Stand

One of my favorite stories is that of the country boys persuading one of their number to allow himself to be hitched up to a small wagon as the teammate of a young yearling steer. The hitched boy said, "Twist his tail. We're balking."

Then the steer started in a reckless run, pulling the boy with him. The boy yelled, "Head us! We are running away!"

Finally they got them stopped, and the other boys started to unhitch the boy from the steer, and he, pointing at the steer, said, "Git him loose. I'll stand!"

The Rev. J. Harold Stephens
SHELBYVILLE, TENNESSEE

Used Hog

There was this city fellow from Huntington who came to a camp in the mountains to spend the summer. After he'd been there a day or two he decided to walk down the road to get acquainted with his neighbor. They visited awhile, then the city fellow asked what he might do with his garbage. His neighbor replied, "Well, I suppose you could bury it, but we just feed ours to the pig." The fellow thought that sounded like a good solution and inquired about where he could get one. The farmer replied that he had just weaned a few and would be happy to sell him one.

He asked fifteen dollars for the pig, and the fellow took it back to camp. He spent the summer relaxing and fishing and enjoying life in the country. As the time approached to return to Huntington, the fellow paid another visit to his neighbor. He said that the pig had worked out just fine and had grown into a great big hog, but he said that he had to leave now and was wondering whether the farmer might want to buy him back.

"Well," said the prudent farmer, "that depends on what you want for him."

The city fellow thought for a moment and said, "Well, I paid you fifteen dollars for him, but I've had the use of him all summer. Would five dollars be too much?"

Unidentified Contributor
WEST VIRGINIA

Whipped Cream is Better

A farmer was hauling manure, and his truck broke down next to a mental institution. One of the patients leaned across the fence and asked, "What are you going to do with that manure?"

The farmer replied, "I'm going to put it on my strawberries."

"We may be crazy," the patient said, "but we put whipped cream on ours."

John Ed McConnell
FRANKFORT, KENTUCKY

Initiative

There was this fellow in town who was not too bright and mostly just hung around. The president of the bank decided to hire him to polish two brass lions at the entrance to the bank, in order to keep him occupied and to provide a little spending money. The man worked diligently at the job for several months and then went to see the president.

He said, "I'm quitting and going into business for myself."

The president was pleased and asked what he was going to do.

The man said, "Well, I've been saving my money, and I've bought two lions of my own."

Dr. James C. Murphy
RICHMOND, KENTUCKY

The Dilemma

There were two small hotels in the town, facing each other. A traveler rides up and addresses the proprietor of one of them:

Traveler: "Say, which one of these hotels is the best?"

Proprietor: "Stranger, no matter which one you go to—you'll wish you'd gone to t'other one."

The late Dr. Josiah H. Combs
PERRY COUNTY, KENTUCKY
AND FT. WORTH, TEXAS

Act of Kindness

A man went into a restaurant and said to the waitress, "I'd like the meatloaf and a few kind words."

The waitress returned and said, "Here's your meatloaf."

He asked, "What about the few kind words?"

She said, "Don't eat the meatloaf."

Judge Ray Corns
FRANKFORT, KENTUCKY

On Second Thought ...

While milking a cow on a hot, humid August evening, a farmer was aggravated by the cow's tail hitting him in the face. He finally tied the cow's tail to his right leg. The farmer said, "Before I had been around the barn seven times, I knew I had made a mistake."

Judge Ray Corns

The Raffle

Farmer A was passing by Farmer B's place, saw a horse he liked, made an offer and bought it. Since Farmer A was going out of town for a couple of days, Farmer B said he would have his boys take the horse to Farmer A's place in his truck. The boys went out for the horse but rushed back to tell their dad that the horse was dead. Farmer B pondered for a moment and said, "Go and pick up that dead horse and deliver him to Farmer A's pasture."

Farmer B expected trouble from Farmer A as soon as he returned home. For days, though, he heard nothing. Finally curiosity got the best of him, and he rode over to Farmer A's place. After some conversation about crops and weather, he inquired, "How is your horse doing?"

Farmer A said, "Would you believe this? I got home and found that horse dead out there in the pasture."

Farmer B said, "I'm terribly sorry to hear that."

Farmer A said, "Oh, that's no problem. I sold chances and raffled off the horse and got more than my money back."

"How in the world could you get away with raffling off a dead horse?" asked Farmer B.

Farmer A said, "Nobody complained except the fellow who won. He raised so much hell I finally gave him his dollar back."

Paul Graham
BENHAM, KENTUCKY

Capital Punishment

There was a woman who went into a pet store and picked out a parrot she wanted to buy. The storeowner said, "Lady, you don't want that parrot."

She said, "Why not?"

"It belonged to a sailor," he said, "and it talks dirty."

She said, "That's all right. I can break it of that habit."

He said, "All right."

She took it home, took the cover off of it, and it started talking dirty and cussing, and so she said, "I'll break you of that habit."

So she grabbed him, threw him in the deep freeze, and closed the door. About twenty minutes later she went back, opened the door, and said, "Now, are you ready to stop that nasty talk?"

He said, "Y-y-e-e-s-s, M-a-a-m-m, b-b-but w-what was it that turkey did?"

> *Billy Wilson*
> BOBTOWN, KENTUCKY

Swallowed Up

The little country school I attended in Harlan County when I was a boy was about a mile and a half from where I lived. Most of the time there would be several of us children traveling this path together. One evening though, I found myself walking home alone. I had just crossed a fence into a cornfield when a slight movement in front of me caught my eye.

Upon looking closer I saw what I took to be a round snake—round like in a circle. As far back as I could remember, I had heard of hoop snakes which didn't crawl like other snakes but rolled on the ground like hoops. The hoopsnake was supposed to have a horn somewhere on it full of deadly poison, and if it rolled up to you and sank its horn in your shin, you were a goner.

I looked for this horn, and not seeing any I ventured up a little closer, enough to see what was going on. To my surprise I saw that two medium-sized gartersnakes were swallowing each other.

Seeing that I was not in dire danger, I sat down nearby to watch, and I saw the circle drawing in on itself, narrowing faster and faster until it met in the middle and touched.

Then right there before my eyes, I saw everything disappear. Both snakes were gone, nothing left. They had completely swallowed each other.

Col. Edward Ward
BLEDSOE, KENTUCKY

Poker-Tail

A tourist stopped by a country store and found three men and a Bluetick hound playing poker.

He said, "Does that dog really understand poker?"

"Yeah, he does," said one of the players, "but he ain't any good at it. Ever' time he gets a good hand, he wags his tail."

Loyal Jones

Packer-Picker

A stranger in a small Kentucky town encountered a boy carrying a banjo.

"Can you play that thing?" he inquired.

"I wouldn't pack 'er if I couldn't pick 'er," the boy replied.

The late Dr. Josiah H. Combs
PERRY COUNTY, KENTUCKY
AND FT. WORTH, TEXAS

Show's Over

A drunk wandered into a subdivision, didn't know where he was or what was going on. He looked over a backyard fence, and there was a homeowner grilling a little chicken on a rotisserie-like device, turning it with his right hand. With his left hand he was putting on Adolf's tenderizer in generous portions. The drunk watched as the smoke got darker and higher, and finally he could stand it no longer.

"Mister," he said, "I hate to tell you, but your music has stopped, and your monkey's all burned up."

Judge Ray Corns
FRANKFORT, KENTUCKY

Who's Left

A bunch of men were digging a hole in the middle of town. The local character who wasn't too smart came by and asked,

"What're you goin' to put in that hole?"

The boss of the job said, "We're going to round up all the sons-of-bitches in town and put them in that hole."

The fellow thought for a minute and then said, "Who's going to cover them up?"

Rev. Will D. Campbell
MT. JULIET, TENNESSEE

Whatever Pleases

A bald man named "Skin" headed a construction crew for an electric cooperative. While supervising a job, he was engaged in conversation by a bystander. Pausing in their talk, the bystander cut a big wedge of chewing tobacco from a plug, and then he offered a piece to Skin, who was known for his abhorrence of tobacco in any form.

He answered emphatically, "No, I'd just as soon go to the chicken house and rake some off the roost and put it in my jaw."

The tobacco chewer considered that statement briefly, spat a streak of ambeer and said, "Well, now, I reckon it's just what a man gets used to."

Hugh Chance
JONESVILLE, VIRGINIA

Good-Looking Suit

I want to tell you about the first suit I ever bought, on Summer Street in Charleston, West Virginia. It was in the late '30s, and I paid eight dollars for it. I was proud as a peacock, walking down the street, looking at myself in store windows, and I bumped into a friend.

I asked him, "What do you think of this suit? I paid eight dollars for it—first one I ever had."

The guy said, "Beautiful suit, but look at that sleeve hanging down over your hand there."

I went back into the store and asked them about it. The clerk said, "You've got a point. Just take that sleeve and pull it up and clamp your elbow down against your side there and no one will ever notice it."

I did that and was walking up the street looking in the windows admiring myself when I bumped into another friend. We went through the same deal.

He said, "Look at that lapel. It's hanging down off your shoulder, not even with the other one."

So I went back in the store and said, "Look I'm a little upset over this whole deal."

The clerk said, "You take this sleeve and hold it like that, and take this lapel and hold it under your chin like this, and nobody will ever notice it."

So I'm walking down the street, and I bump into another friend, and I just said, "New suit. Eight bucks."

He said, "What about the seat of the pants?"

I went back in the store and said, "Look, I'm pretty sick of this. I paid good money, and there ought to be a warranty or something ... "

"Well, you've got a point," the man said, "but I'll tell you what you can do. Pull that sleeve up there and hold it, take your chin and hold this lapel, and take your two fingers and thumb and pull up the crotch like this, and no one will ever notice."

So, I was walking down the street and came to the curb, having some trouble getting off the curb holding my suit like that. Standing nearby were two medical students. One said to the other, "Look at that guy. He must have been in a terrible car accident or something."

The other one said, "Yeah, but ain't that a heck of a good-looking suit!"

George Daugherty
ELKVIEW, WEST VIRGINIA

Doesn't Look

A man in Sneedville, Tennessee, was looking at a brood sow. The owner offered it for sale at a very reasonable price, considering its size.

"What's wrong with her?" the prospective buyer asked.

"Well, she just don't look too good," he replied.

"Looks all right to me. I'll take her."

On unloading the sow at his place, the buyer found that she was completely blind.

When he saw the man who sold her, he said, "That sow you sold me is blind as a bat."

He said, "Well, I told you when you bought her that she didn't look too good."

Hugh Chance
JONESVILLE, VIRGINIA

That Is, If You Want To

Some say that if you play heavy metal music backwards, you get Satanic messages. If you play country music backwards, you sober up, and get your job, house and wife back.

Tom Skidmore
BEREA, KENTUCKY

Not Speaking

A fellow was driving along and saw a farmer plowing his corn with a mule. When he reached the end of each row, he'd jerk the mule's lines to stop him, yank him around, and then hit him with the end of the line to get him going again.

The fellow stopped and called to the farmer, "Why don't you teach that mule 'get-up' and 'whoa,' and 'gee' and 'haw.' "

The farmer said, "Oh, he knows all of that, but the son-of-a-bitch kicked me a minute ago, and I'm not speaking to him."

Ken Davis
BEREA, KENTUCKY

Gone in Style

Two fellows grew up in eastern Kentucky. One went off to make his fortune up North, while the other stayed home to run the farm and take care of the old folks. The one who went north prospered, went up in his company, was transferred to California, became president. He never came back home for a visit he was so busy.

One day the one back home sent a wire, "Papa died. Funeral on Friday." The one in California wired back "Can't come. Must go to Japan for merger with big Japanese company. Give Papa very best funeral, and send bill to me. Least I can do."

So they buried Papa, and the company president got a bill for $5,000. He paid it, and a month later he got a bill for $100. Thinking that something had been forgotten, he paid that too, but the next month there was another bill for $100. He paid it. Third month, another $100 bill. So he called his brother and said, "What are those $100 bills for?"

His brother said, "Well, you indicated you wanted Papa buried in style, so I rented him a tuxedo."

J. Richard Carleton
GEORGETOWN, KENTUCKY

EDUCATION:

When You Can't Afford It, You Learn To Use Your Head

Learning Never Ends

Two men were talking, and one said, "What is your son going to be when he gets out of college?"

The other one said, "Senile."

Judge Ray Corns
FRANKFORT, KENTUCKY

Long-Range Planning

A third-grade teacher wanted her children to start thinking of their future, and one day she said, "I want you children to think of what you want to be or do when you become an adult. Put it in the form of a little verse. When you are all finished, we'll let you stand and recite it." The first little boy got up and recited,

> *My name is Dan,*
> *And when I become a man*
> *I'd like to be emperor of Japan*
> *If I can,*
> *And I think I can.*

A little girl got up and recited,

My name is Sadie
And when I become a lady
I would like to have a baby
If I can
And I think I can.

A third student, a boy, stood up and said,

My name is Sam. Unlike Dan,
I don't want to be emperor of Japan.
I much prefer Sadie's plan
And I want to help her if I can
And I think I can.

Judge Ray Corns

Asexual Education

Parents of a schoolboy asked him if he had sex education in school.

He said, "Yes, we did. First, the preacher came and told us not to do it, the nurse came and told us how not to do it, and then the principal came and told us where not to do it."

Loyal Jones

Making Do

A professor who had just gotten his Ph.D. from the university was driving down a country road when his car conked out.

After he'd fruitlessly tried to start it for some time, a grizzled old farmer plowing in a nearby field walked over, pulled a few wires, and it started.

"That's amazing," said the professor. "Here I am a Ph.D., and I couldn't start this car, and yet you, a man of obviously little formal education, knew exactly what to do."

"Doctor," the farmer said, "when you can't afford a lot of education, you learn to use your head."

Mrs. S. J. Stokes, Sr.
LEXINGTON, KENTUCKY

Getting it Straight

In the Kentucky hills, a first grade teacher had taken her class out for recess and organized games for a footrace. The little boy who won came across the finish line with loud shouts, "Me won! Me won! Me won!"

The teacher felt compelled to discharge her teaching duties and took the little fellow by the shoulders and said, "No, I won. I won."

The little boy quickly replied, "Hell no you didn't! You didn't even run!"

Gail Boots Diederich
ODESSA, FLORIDA

Pareful

While teaching in a rural school in east Tennessee, I was assigned to the kindergarten level. Little John, the son of a timber cutter, was a rather slow learner and seldom came up with the correct answer.

It was the week before Easter, and I was going over words that they might encounter during the Easter holidays. John paid little attention until we came to the word parasol. Then he brightened and his hand shot up. Of course, with delight I asked John to tell the class what a parasol was.

"It's what you saw down trees with," he replied.

Gail Boots Diederich

Lass or Grass

The last story reminds me of when I arranged for two Chicago social workers at a workshop to live with some people in eastern Kentucky for the week-end. The host was down in his back and in bad shape. So they asked him what happened. He said "Well it was my pare mooer." He meant power mower, but they thought he said paramour. So they took great interest when he described the situation.

He said, "Well I got me a pare mooer and, Buddy, we went round and round. Wasn't no time 'til I got down in my back so bad I had to go to the doctor. He said, 'You got to get rid of that pare mooer!' "

Loyal Jones

Elephant Memory

An old biology teacher had always given the same question on every final exam since he began teaching. It was, "Describe the anatomy, morphology, and habitat of the elephant." So, this student who wasn't too swift, had prepared himself for this question. But when he got the exam, to his horror, the professor had changed it to read, "Describe the anatomy, morphology, and habitat of the flea."

He sat for a long time and then began, "The flea is a tiny creature which often lives on elephants. The elephant is large mammal ..."

Dr. Smith T. Powell
BEREA, KENTUCKY

Moist Mouse

A little girl came home from her one-room school, and her mother asked her what had happened at school that day.

She said, "Well, not much, except that I watched a little mouse run around the schoolroom, and it finally ran up our teacher's leg. She grabbed it through her dress tail and squeezed it as hard as she could. I never knew you could squeeze that much water out of a mouse."

Carl J. Carlson
DELAVAN, WISCONSIN

The Bastard Case

A professor was hard-nosed about facts and often embarrassed students in class when they could not back up their opinions. One girl had answered a question and the professor asked, "Do you have evidence for that statement?"

She said, "No, I don't."

He said, "Well until you provide it, may we call you a liar?"

She asked, "Professor, do you have a birth certificate?"

He said, "No, not with me."

She asked, "Then may we consider you a bastard until you produce one?"

> *Jane Winstead*
> SNEEDVILLE, TENNESSEE

Home Schooling

A father was trying to help his son with his math homework. "What's two from two?" the son asked.

The father explained, "Well, if I gave you two apples and then took both of them away, how many would you have?"

"Nary a one, Paw," he answered.

"That's right," said the father. "Put down nary."

> *Judge Russell Dunbar*
> HUNTINGTON, WEST VIRGINIA

Fotch and Brung

Byron Crawford, columnist for the *Louisville Courier-Journal* tells of a little boy who put an apple on his teacher's desk before she entered the room. Seeing the apple she inquired about it. The little boy jumped up and said, "I fotched it!" Then he paused, thought a minute and said, "Looky thar! I said fotched when I meant to say brung!"

> *Byron Crawford*
> WARSAW, KENTUCKY

High Maintenance

An industrial school was being founded at Hindman, in Knott County. The ladies delegated to start the school were from the lowlands. The trip from the railway station, at Jackson, required two days in order to reach Hindman, and the ladies were traveling in a jolt-wagon, over rough, dirt roads. They stopped at a mountaineer's home the first night. The beds were in one room. The mountaineer's wife watched, with great curiosity, the ladies undress and put on their sleeping garments before retiring.

"Do ye all do this every night before ye go to bed?" she asked them. On being told that they did, she paused for several seconds, then said, "Ye all must be a lot o' trouble to yeselves."

The late Josiah H. Combs
PERRY COUNTY, KENTUCKY,
AND FT. WORTH TEXAS

She Asked

There was a second grade teacher trying to teach spelling and arithmetic. She was working on the word "feet." Agatha was having trouble. The teacher said, "Now, Agatha, what do I have two of that cows have four of?" And Agatha told her.

Lonnie "Pap" Wilson
NASHVILLE, TENNESSEE

Off the Old Block

The teacher asked my boy Johnnie which one of his parents he favored, and he couldn't answer, so he came home and asked his mother. She replied, "You just tell her that you have your father's features but your eyes are like mine."

Little Johnnie was hardly in the school the next morning when he made himself heard, "I can answer your question now, Teacher. My eyes are like my mother's, but I have my father's fixtures."

Lonnie "Pap" Wilson

Pee Protocol

A third grade teacher told her class on the first day of school,

"If any of you need to go to the bathroom, just hold up two fingers like this."

A little boy on the back row said, "I don't see how that's going to help a bit."

Judge Ray Corns
FRANKFORT, KENTUCKY

Censored Feedback

The teacher asked one of her students what his father thought of his report card.

"Shall I leave out the cuss-words?" he asked.

"Yes, of course."

"Well, he didn't say nothin'."

The late Raymond Layne
BEREA, KENTUCKY

Academic In Decision

Once after a shipwreck this college president found himself stuck with two preachers on a small deserted island in the South Seas.

After a few days of this lonely isolation the three were growing desperate when, lo and behold, a bottle washed up to shore. The president picked up the bottle and rubbed off the surf scum, trying to see if there might be a note in there. Suddenly a geni appeared out of the bottle.

"I am at your service," the geni said. "I can give one of you three wishes, or all of you one wish."

They decided to spread the good fortune around and take one wish apiece, so a preacher went first. "I wish I were back with my congregation," he said, and *poof!* he was gone.

The next preacher said, "I miss my wife so much, I wish I were back home with her." *Poof!* He was gone too.

Now it was the college president's turn, so the geni said, "Now, sir, what is your wish?"

The president said, "You know, it's very hard for me to make a decision on my own. I sure wish those two guys were back here with me."

Dr. John B. Stephenson,
PRESIDENT EMERITUS,
BEREA COLLEGE, BEREA, KENTUCKY

Sign of the Times

I had a teacher from Salyersville in Magoffin County who was going to be a nun until she "cooked her habit," as she put it. But she had a class in reading, and she told us children, "You don't have to write or talk sometimes to get your point across." By way of example she stuck out her thumb and asked us, "What does this mean?"

We all said, "I want a ride."

Then she asked, "What does this mean?" (She held her finger up across her mouth.)

We said, "Be quiet."

Then she asked a child, "What can you say using signs?" (He held up his hand flat to say *stop*.)

Then finally she asked this one little boy to do one, and he gave the Catholic sign of crossing your chest and touching your forehead. That just thrilled her because she once thought of becoming a nun.

She said, "Jerry, what does that mean?"

He said, "That means I'm gonna shoot a free throw."

Charlie Tribble
CYNTHIANA, KENTUCKY

Back Like He Was

One of the less brilliant boys of a rural community was kicked in the head by a mule. After a while, he seemed to have recovered. A neighbor asked the boy's father if his son had gotten all right.

"No," said the father, "he didn't get all right, but he did get back to like he was."

Rev. J. Harold Stephens
SHELBYVILLE, TENNESSEE

Hillbilly Deductive Reasoning

I had trouble in high school, couldn't read real well, so they decided to give me an oral test. I'd been there about six years in high school, and they wanted to get rid of me, and I wanted to get out. So they called me in and said, "We have three questions for you, and if you can answer these to our satisfaction, you will be able to graduate."

I asked, "Well, what are they?"

The first question was: How many seconds are there in a year? I said, "You've got to be kidding. That's a math question, and if I'm worse in anything other than reading, it's math! But, if you'll give me twenty-four hours, I'll try to figure it out."

The second question was: Name two days that start with a T. I said, "Man, another tough question! Can you give me some time to figure that one out, too?" They said yes.

The third question was: How many D's in "Rudolph The Red-Nosed Reindeer"? I said, "Oh, no, another math question. But if you'll give me twenty-four hours I'll try to figure out the answers to all three questions."

I don't think I slept any that night trying to figure out those three questions.

Well, we met again the next day and they asked, "How many seconds are there in a year?" I said, "As far as I can figure, there's twelve." They asked me how I arrived at that. I said, "Well, there's Jan. 2, Feb. 2, Mar. 2 ..."

They said, "Well, that wasn't the answer we had anticipated, but we'll count that one right."

Then they asked me to name two days that start with a T. I said, "Today and Tomorrow." They allowed they'd count that one right too, so I figured I was on my way.

The third question they asked me was how many D's in "Rudolph the Red-Nosed Reindeer." I told them I counted them many times last night and the answer I came up with was 167. They looked at each other and then asked me, "How did you arrive at that?"

I said, "Well," (singing) "de-de de de de de-de, de-de de-de de de de ..."

John Holbrook
ROCKCASTLE COUNTY, KENTUCKY

Erudite Animals

When I came to Berea I worked in the library, because I knew it was important that I get close to books. One day a chicken came in there, walked up to the desk and said, "Boo-ok-k-k-k," so, I gave it a book. I hadn't been there long, but I could understand that much.

The next day, it came back and walked up to the desk and said, "Boo-ok-k-k-k, Boo-ok-k-k-k." So I gave it two books.

Now, the third day it was back there again, and I knew I had a good reader on my hands. This time it said, "Boo-ok-k-k-k, Boo-ok-k-k-k, Boo-ok-k-k-k," so I gave it three books.

I knew it was unusual for chickens to come in and check out books, so I decided to follow that chicken. I followed it across U.S. 25, down by the President's home and through the garden, and then it disappeared down behind a big tree there on Silver Creek.

I got up close and looked behind that tree, and sure enough, that chicken had propped up one of those books and appeared to be reading it.

Just then, a frog came up out of the creek and looked at the chicken. The chicken looked at the frog and said, "Boo-ok-k-k-k," and the frog said, "Read-it, read-it."

John Holbrook

Shallow Water

There was a little boy named Johnny, and one day the teacher told his class to write a rhyme. So that night Johnny worked real hard on his class assignment.

The next day the teacher asked Johnny to get up and read his rhyme to the class, and he said OK. And this is what he wrote:

I went down to the river to take a swim.

I took off my shirt and hung it on a limb.
I took off my britches and laid them in the grass.
I jumped into the water up to my ... knees.
The teacher said, "Johnny, that's nice, but it doesn't rhyme."
Johnny said, "Well, it would have if the water had been deeper."

Heather Reynolds
BEREA, KENTUCKY

Loose Lung

A mother took her son to buy a sweater. He wanted a turtleneck collar, but she thought he should get one with a V-neck. He resisted, so she asked him why he didn't want a V-neck.

"Well," he said, "my teacher was wearing one, and when she leaned down to help me with my math, one of her lungs fell out."

Paul Neal
BANNER ELK, NORTH CAROLINA

Slim Profit Margin

I work down in Rio Grande, Ohio, about fourteen miles from the Ohio River, and we have a lot of West Virginians come through that part of the country. A couple of them, Clem and Zeke, got into the business of buying and selling hay. They would come across the river, buy hay at fifty cents per bale, and take it back to West Virginia to sell it there for fifty cents a bale.

They didn't make any money on the deal but they couldn't figure out why.

They got to studying about it, got some calculators and computers, and hired some consultants. They all put their heads together and figured and worked and figured.

Finally they decided that they needed a bigger truck.

Ivan Tribe
MCARTHUR, OHIO

See Saw Seen

A hobo went up to a fashionable house to seek a handout. A fine looking lady came to the door, and he asked for food or money.

"Young man, did you see that pile of wood out there that needs sawing?" she said.

"Yeah, I seen it," the man said.

"Your English is terrible," she said. "You should have said, 'I saw it.' "

He said, "You saw me see it, but you ain't seen me saw it."

David Burgio
BEREA, KENTUCKY

Gooses

The following story was part of an address made by the Honorable John E. Garner to the Clark County, Kentucky, Historical Society, March 13, 1923.

Poole was the only tailor here, and he and his son quarreled all the time at each other, and I heard a story about one time they decided to buy some smoothing irons, which is an iron with a fire inside of it and is called a tailor's goose. He wanted two of them, and he asked his son to write to Edwards and Son for a tailor's goose, or rather two of them, and he wrote, "Please send me two tailor's gooses."

The old man found fault with that, and they quarreled about it for a while, and then the son wrote, "Please send me two tailor's geese. The old man fumed violently about this, and the son, becoming angry, refused to write any more.

Then the old man sat down and composed a letter which read, "Edwards and Son: Please send me one tailor's goose, and damn it, send me another one just like it."

The Honorable John E. Garner
WINCHESTER, KENTUCKY

Don't Forget the Condominiums

A sixth grade boy was asked by his father if he was receiving sex education at school, and he said he was.

"What have you learned?" his father asked.

"Well, I've learned to buy condominiums and to avoid intersections," he said.

Dr. Noel Stephens
BEREA, KENTUCKY

Is "Cluck" Past or Present Tense?

I don't know a lot about grammar. For example, I get mixed up on "lay" or "lie." The other day, one of my old hens cackled, and I didn't know whether she had laid or lied.

Verna Mae Slone
PIPPA PASSES, KENTUCKY

Chemistry

A college chemistry teacher asked on a quiz what the greatest advancement in chemistry had been over the last hundred years"

"Blondes," wrote one student.

Loyal Jones

Moveable Dog

A policeman called into the station and said, "There's a dead dog on Willihatchie Street."

The dispatcher asked, "How do you spell Willihatchie?"

The policeman said, "I'll call you back."

In a little while he called back and said, "That dead dog's on Lee Street."

Bernie Peace
WHEELING, WEST VIRGINIA

COURT AND SPARK:

The Comedy of Eros

A Report on Sex from Heaven

Joe and Barney were best friends all their lives. One of their promises to each other was that whoever died first would come back and tell the other one what heaven was like.

Barney died first, in his mid seventies, and one night he came back while Joe was sleeping. "Joe," he said, "this is Barney."

"Barney! You're back! Quick, tell me what it's like."

"Well," said Barney, "I get up in the morning, have breakfast, and then I have sex until noon. Then I eat a nice lunch, take a nap, and then have sex the rest of the afternoon. After that I eat supper and have some more sex, and then I go to sleep."

"So that's what heaven is like," Joe said in wonder.

"I'm not in heaven," said Barney. "I'm a jack rabbit in West Texas."

Chinquapin Jones
GRAVEL SWITCH, KENTUCKY

A Fashioned-Minded Old Man

The ninety-three-year-old East Kentucky man, who had been having some prostate trouble, looked extremely worried when the doctor told him he thought the best course of action would be to remove his testicles.

"Can't I keep at least one of 'em, Doc?" the proud mountain

man pleaded earnestly.

"Naw, I think it'd be better if we took them both out, Mr. Leatherwood," the doctor said firmly.

The old man took a deep breath and let it out slowly, shaking his head. He looked sad enough to cry.

"Now come on, Mr. Leatherwood," the doctor persisted. "You're ninety-three years old. What's the big deal? You don't need them anymore."

"Yeah, maybe so, Doc," the old man replied as he straightened up, regaining a slight twinkle in his eye, "but they sure do dress a man up!"

The late C. H. "Coach" Wyatt
BEREA, KENTUCKY

Q & A from Male/Female Perspective

Q: (Man) What's the difference between a wife and a mistress?
A: About forty-five pounds.
Q: (Woman) What's the difference between a husband and a lover?
A: About forty-five minutes.

Chinquapin Jones
GRAVEL SWITCH, KENTUCKY

Biblical Bickering

Most TV evangelists bore me but I learned something the other night. This preacher said there was substantiation in the Bible for PMS. He said, "Mary rode Joseph's ass all the way to Bethlehem!"

John Jarrard
NASHVILLE, TENNESSEE

Good Match

A traveling salesman stopped at a remote farmhouse and asked to spend the night. The farmer said, "Yes, we'll be glad to have you, but you'll have to sleep with that red-headed schoolteacher."

The salesman said, "That's all right. I'm a gentleman."

The farmer said, "Good. So is he."

Lonnie "Pap" Wilson
NASHVILLE, TENNESSEE

An Elk Built for Two

When I grew up in Elkview, West Virginia, we didn't have the motorcycles that you see these kids running around on today, you know, these boys a-roaring around with girls up behind them, and their arms around their tummy. It looks like so much fun it makes me green with envy.

We had no such thing up at Elkview. Back then you had to take a girlfriend home on a mule or a pony from Wednesday night prayer meeting, or whatever you might have. I had an elk myself.

One Wednesday night I talked this beautiful young lady into going home with me after prayer meeting. She jumped up behind me on the elk, put her arms around my waist, hands around my tummy, and I put my hands up on the elk's antlers and we were just flying up Elk River. All at once she said, "My hands are cold."

I never gave it a thought when I said, "Just put them down in my overall pockets. It'll be all right."

Lo and behold, I had forgotten that my mother had neglected to mend that hole in my right hand pants pocket. So directly she said, "Well, what in the world is *that?*"

Thinking very quickly, like us boys up at Elkview do, I said, "That's my chewing tobacco."

She said, "You're just about *out,* ain't ye, buddy?"

George Daugherty
ELKVIEW, WEST VIRGINIA

George, a lawyer in West Virginia, is known as "The Earl of Elkview." An all around entertainer, he is also a songwriter, an actor, storyteller, and saw player who was a regular on National Public Radio's "Mountain Stage."

Desire at Midnight

When I was chief counsel for the Kentucky Department of Education, it came time for the receptionist to retire after thirty years. I said to my secretary, "Check around and see what would be a nice present for me to get her."

She came back and said that the receptionist liked perfume, a special perfume called "Desire at Midnight." The next time I was in Cincinnati, I went up to the second floor of a big department store. There was a very typical type of lady behind the counter—about sixty-five years old, 18-18-18, a professional model for a dipstick. I'm not being critical, just setting the scene. She was wearing every type of cosmetic they sold. She looked like Tammy Faye Baker with a paint roller. She'd had her face lifted so many times that if she sneezed her shoes would have flown off. I sauntered up, going to ask her about something that I knew nothing about.

"Pardon me Ma'am, but do you have Desire at Midnight?"

And she said, "Oh, no sir, I have to drink coffee to stay up for the ten o'clock news."

Judge Ray Corns
FRANKFORT, KENTUCKY

Deficit Lover

I told Dad, "Dad, you know that girl I'm in love with? Well, I think she's chasing me just for my money!"

Dad said, "Son, you don't have any money."

I said, "I know, she's stupid, too!"

Johnny Hylton
BEREA, KENTUCKY

Super Soup

The older man opened the door of his motel room to find an attractive young lady, scantily clad, smiling at him.

"I'm here to give you a good time tonight," she said. "Whatever your heart desires."

"There must be some mistake," the man said. "I didn't call

for a woman."

She said, "Well, somebody did, somebody who likes you and wanted to surprise you. So here I am. And I'm good, darlin'. If you'll let me come in I'll give you super sex."

The man thought a minute, looked at the lady, and said, "If it's all the same with you, I'll just take the soup."

Ewel Cornett
LOUISVILLE, KENTUCKY

Old Grandpa Can Still Boogie

A friend of mine told me his Granddad, who was about eighty-three, got married again, this time to a twenty-three-year-old girl. He said his Granddad was getting kind of feeble, but he still liked to make love a lot, so at about ten in the morning this friend would go over to his Granddad's and help position him on top of his wife. Then at about two in the afternoon he and his brother would go over and take the old man off.

I asked him, "How come you can put him on by yourself, but it takes two of you to get him back off?"

He said, "Oh, he'll fight ye!"

Chet Atkins, C.G.P.
NASHVILLE, TENNESSEE

Half-Life

Two married women were discussing life in the hereafter. "Does your husband believe in life after death?" one asked the other.

"Heck, no," said the other. "He doesn't even believe in life after supper."

Mary Forcht
LOUISVILLE, KENTUCKY

The Proof

When my brother and I were little boys, we were playing on the floor, and my brother looked up at our mother and asked, "Mama, how old are you?" She said, "Son, you're not supposed to ask a lady her age. Go on back to playing."

In a little while he said, "Mama, how much do you weigh?" She said, "That's not something you ought to ask a lady. Go on and play."

He played a while and asked, "Mama, what were you and Daddy fussing about in your bedroom last night?" She said, "Son, that's none of your business. Go about your own business and play."

In a little while my brother sneaked upstairs, and he came back holding her driver's license and said, "Mama, I've found the answer to all my questions. It says here you are twenty-nine, you weigh 115 pounds, and you got an F in sex."

Marc Pruett
ASHEVILLE, NORTH CAROLINA

Welfare Case

A trust officer in a bank which usually handled large accounts was stuck with the $10,000 trust of a maiden lady because she had been a relative of somebody in the bank. The trust was to assure that she had a proper burial when she died, but she came in once a month and took up a lot of time inquiring about how her investments were doing.

One day she came in and said that she thought $5,000 was adequate for her burial and that she would like to spend the rest on an experience she'd never had, a night with a man. She asked the trust officer to think about how this might be accomplished. That evening over dinner, he mentioned the strange request to his wife. She said, "Well, you know you have been hoping we could save enough money to remodel the house."

"Oh no, he said. I couldn't do that. It wouldn't be right. I'm a professional trust officer."

But she kept pestering him and thought it might be a solution to the problems of both parties, so he finally agreed to do it. He called the lady, and she agreed for him to come to her house that very evening. She lived out in the country, and so he asked his wife to drive him out. When they got there, he said, "Now I don't think this is a good idea, but I'll do it. I want you here in the morning at 7:30 in the morning to pick me up. Don't be late."

The next morning she drove out and parked in front of the woman's house before the appointed time. She waited, and waited, but he didn't come out. So, she blew her horn. A window went up in an upstairs room, and her husband leaned out and said, "Come back at 7:30 tomorrow morning. She's decided to let the county bury her."

James MacNeal
HAMILTON, OHIO

Change of Schedule

This old guy got up and shaved one morning, came out and said to his wife, "Boy, that makes me feel twenty years younger."

His wife said, "Did you ever think of shaving at night?"

Billy Edd Wheeler

That, or Restraint

A woman who had fourteen children was asked what quality she most admired in a man.

"Moderation," she said.

Loyal Jones

Paranoid

A man went to see a psychiatrist about his wife.

"What's the matter with her," the doctor asked.

"Why, she's got this phobia that somebody's going to steal her clothes."

"What makes you think that?" the psychiatrist persisted.

"Well, I came home early the other day and found a man sitting in her closet to guard them."

Loyal Jones

Clean Fun

I took this beautiful woman out one night in Elkview, and on the way to dinner I asked if she'd like to have a cigarette, and I thought she was going to slap my face! When we got to the restaurant, I asked her if she would like a drink before dinner, and boy, she said, "Lips that touch liquor will never touch mine."

Well, I thought, "We're in for a big evening!" But on the way home, we were going by the Elkview Hilton, and I said, "Let's just go in here and spend the night."

She said, "Why, that would be lovely."

Well, the next morning, we were on our way home, and I said, "I don't understand you. You got terribly agitated when I offered you a cigarette, and you almost smacked my face when I offered you a drink, but when I mentioned spending the night at the Hilton, you were all smiles."

She said, "Well, it's like I've been telling my Sunday School class, you don't have to drink and smoke to have a good time!"

George Daugherty
ELKVIEW, WEST VIRGINIA

A Taste of Tobacco

There was a young fellow, about seventeen, who sat down on the davenport with his girlfriend. They smooched for about forty-five minutes, had a wonderful time, and then he backed off and said, "When I sat down here, Dear, was you a-chewing tobacco, or was I?"

George Daugherty

Form Letter

A fellow got a letter from a man accusing him of running around with his wife. The letter said, "Meet me Saturday morning at my office and we will settle this thing once and for all."

The man wrote back and said, "I got your form letter. Sorry I can't make the meeting, but whatever you and the other fellows decide is all right with me."

John Ed McConnell
FRANKFORT, KENTUCKY

Bonus

This fellow went to a house of ill repute and said, "Is Myrtle in?"

The madam said, "Yes, she is. Go right on up."

He went on up, greeted Myrtle, pulled out $200 and asked, "Will this be sufficient?"

She said, "Oh yes, indeed." He made love to her and really pleased her.

The next night he came back with $200 more. Same thing. She was so pleased with him that she said, "Look, I'm attracted to you. You are really different. Let's go on a picnic. It'll be my treat."

He said, "I can't. I have to go back to Atlanta."

She said, "Oh, I have a sister in Atlanta."

He said, "I know, she gave me that $400 to give to you."

Bob Hannah
ATLANTA, GEORGIA

HORMONES
A Song by Chet Atkins, C.G.P. & Billy Edd Wheeler

A feller out in Arkansas hit the campaign trail
He said he'd had a puff or two, but he didn't inhale
Then he stopped to smell the Flowers, 'least that's what I read
He said he didn't do it, but that's not what Jennifer said.

Chorus:
She said his hormones got to strollin', a-rockin' & a rollin'
She said he didn't mean to be unkind
His hormones were just working overtime.

Then there was the Donald, the trump card of them all
Who bought himself a shuttle and a little ole Taj Mahal
Then he took a notion to take a skiiing trip
Among the Aspens and the maples, thought he'd try a double dip.

Chorus:
Their hormones went skedaddle, the trainer won the battle

He's the best there is at kiss-and-tell
And the book they wrote is selling very well.

Poor Jim went to prison making eighty cents a day
At first he didn't mind it 'cause he had Tammy Faye
But her hormones started working and she dropped him real quick
Now poor old Jim remembers ... how she stood by him through
thick.

Chorus:
Her hormones started workin', workin' and a-jerkin'
Tammy didn't mean to be unkind
Her hormones were just working overtime.

Lisa Marie and Michael called the Reverend to their pad
Priscilla tried to stop her, but she said I love him bad
She said we're both determined and want to marry soon
The preacher stared in wonder, said "Which one's the groom?"

Chorus:
Their hormones got to talkin', talkin' and moonwalkin'
Elvis did a flip-flop in his grave
But sometimes those old hormones won't behave.

Bridge/Tag:
Talking 'bout hormones, them crazy little hormones
They've snuck up on a few good friends of mine
Those hormones get to strollin', get to rockin' and a-rollin'
Those hormones just love working overtime!

* * *

FAMILY RELATIONS:

Men Tell Us What To Do, And We Tell Them Where To Go

Found at Last

Just when this man was getting to sleep, his wife shook him and said, "I hear someone downstairs."

So, he got his shotgun and went creeping down the stairs. He turned on the light, and sure enough there was a burglar, sacking up their valuables. Pointing the shotgun at him, the husband said, "Stay right there until I call my wife. She's been waiting for you for forty years."

Rev. John Sherfey
STANLEY, VIRGINIA

Imagine a Solution

Another woman woke her husband to tell him that she couldn't sleep because she thought there was a mouse under their bed. He said, "Well, just start thinking there is also a cat under the bed and go to sleep."

Loyal Jones

No Easy Task

A fellow came home drunk with a bottle of cheap whiskey in his hand. His wife met him at the door and said, "Since you think that stuff is so great, I'll just join you."

She took the bottle, took a big swig, gasped, choked and gagged.

He said, "There, I'll bet you thought I was enjoying that stuff all these years."

Loyal Jones

Nowhere-Bound

A little girl got mad at her parents, packed her clothes, and started to leave home. Her father asked, "Where are you going?"

"That's the hell of it," she said. "I just don't know."

The late Mace Crandall
BEREA, KENTUCKY

Sinker

I took my grandson, Mitchell Aldridge, for a swimming lesson. He was scared and said, "Be careful. I drown easy."

Shirley Jones
MARBLE, NORTH CAROLINA

Shank's Mare

A senior in high school came to his father and proposed that he buy him a car. The father said he would if he made all A's and B's on his next report card and got a haircut. He brought home his next report card with all A's and B's, but he hadn't cut his hair. His father pointed this out, but he said, "Well, in all those pictures I've seen of Jesus, He had long hair."

His father said, "Yes, and as I remember, He walked everywhere He went."

Loyal Jones

House Husband

A hen-pecked husband was very disappointed when his wife had a baby daughter. He was hoping for a boy to help him with the housework.

Loyal Jones

History Buff

One man said to his friend, "Was your wife mad at you when you got home so late last night?"

"Yes," he replied, "she was plumb historical."

"Don't you mean hysterical?"

"No, historical. She brought up things that happened forty years ago."

The late Honorable Brooks Hays
LITTLE ROCK, ARKANSAS

Conservative

A woman told her husband that she had always wanted a milkbath and asked him if he would arrange one for her birthday. He said he would. On her birthday, he went to a local dairy and told the manager that he wanted enough milk for a bath.

"Do you want it pasteurized?" the man asked.

After reflection, he said, "No, I think just up around her armpits will be about right."

Loyal Jones

Choosier

A mother of three really unruly children was asked whether she'd have children if she had it to do over again.

"Yes," she said, "but not the same ones."

Reva Welch
JEFFERSONTOWN, KENTUCKY

News Item

A woman whose husband had left her for another woman decided to commit suicide. She jumped out of a third-story window. She was rushed to the hospital and is doing well. However, her husband on whom she landed, died on the spot.

Nina Jones Cotton
SIERRA VISTA, ARIZONA

Shut off the Light

An old doctor went to a mountain home to deliver a baby. Since the house had no electricity and only one kerosene lamp, he asked for more light, and the husband went out to the barn and got a lantern. The doctor asked him to bring the lantern over to the bed and hold it so he could see. He delivered a baby, spanked it, it cried, and he said, "We got a good, healthy baby here."

The husband looked the baby over and took the lantern over to the corner of the room. The doctor said, "Bring that lantern back over here." He went back to work and delivered another baby, held it up and said, "We got twins here." The husband took the light back over in the corner.

In a few minutes, the doctor said, "Bring that light back over here. I think there may be another one."

The husband said, "I ain't a-going to do it. I think it's the light that attracting them."

Loyal Jones

Wrong Number

A wealthy farmer called home while on a trip. The hired girl answered. He said, "Let me speak to my wife."

The girl said, "She can't come to the phone. She's in bed with your best friend."

Of course he was upset. He said, "Take my gun and go shoot both of them."

Blam! Blam! he heard on the phone and the maid came back and said, "I did it."

"What did you do with the gun?" he asked.

"I threw it in the swimming pool."

"Swimming pool?" he shouted. "Is this 459-3232?"

Loyal Jones

No Sweat

Bill said to his girlfriend, "Darling, I think I ought to tell you that I am seeing a psychiatrist."

She said, "Why, that's all right. I'm seeing a psychiatrist, your cousin, and a bulldozer operator."

Loyal Jones

Poor Math

A man persisted in calling his wife "Mother of Six." She didn't like it.

One night at a party he said, "Let's go home, Mother of Six." She said, "OK, Father of Four."

Loyal Jones

Big Clarence

A girl lived at home with six big brothers, and when she got to be eighteen, she said she was leaving, and so she went to Norfolk, met a sailor and married him. After a month or so she came home with a black eye. Her father asked about it and she said, "Clarence did it."

The father was upset, but she said that she and Clarence were working on it. A few weeks later she came home again with another black eye and said Clarence had done it but that they were working on their problems. The father vowed to himself that if this happened again, he and the boys would go over and teach Clarence a lesson. In a few more weeks the daughter came home with two black eyes.

"This is it," said the father, and he rounded up his boys, put them in the back of his pickup and headed for Norfolk. He got on the interstate, drove a few miles and went under an overpass, threw on his brakes, did a U-turn across the median and headed back toward home. His boys started beating on the cab, and he slowed down and opened his window.

"Why are we going back, Pa?"

"Didn't you see that sign on that overpass, said 'Clarence eight feet, four inches?'"

Craig Williams
BEREA, KENTUCKY

Economy

A woman lost her husband, and she decided to put a statement in the newspaper. She wrote out a nice piece, but the lady at the newspaper told her that it would cost a dollar a word, and she said she couldn't afford that. The lady told her that she could just put in a notice. So she said put in "Mike died."

The lady said, "You can have three more words for the same price."

She said, "Mike died. Volkswagen for sale."

Lily McGinty
PROSPECT, KENTUCKY

Pretty Far

When my wife and I got married, I got a brother-in-law in the deal at no extra cost. His name is Walden, but we call him Waldo. He's the type of fellow about whom it might be said, "When his time came to drink from the Fountain of Knowledge, he only gargled."

He had to go to Columbus, Ohio, for a few days. His car wasn't working, so he caught the bus. He'd not traveled extensively, so he'd never see a female cab driver. He caught a taxi from the bus station to go to a state office in Columbus, and he got into a cab driven by a young lady.

"How far do you want to go?" she asked Waldo.

His case comes up next Tuesday.

Judge Ray Corns
FRANKFORT, KENTUCKY

Foggy Headed

A businessman who was supposed to be away from home all week on a business trip came home unexpectedly on a Thursday night, a day early. He and his wife went to bed, and the telephone rang. He picked it up, listened for a minute and then said, "How in the heck should I know? Call the Coast Guard!"

His wife asked, "Who was that?"

He said, "Oh, it was some fool, wanted to know if the coast was clear."

Judge Ray Corns

Might be the Wrong Man

I was sitting at Maynor's store in Elkview, and a feller came by and said, "You know, when I came home last night, my wife told me she was expecting, and I thought, 'My Lord, that's our eighteenth child!' So, I went over this morning and got up on the Elkview Bridge, goin' to jump off and kill myself."

Somebody said, "Well, thank Heavens, you didn't."

"Well," he said, "I got to thinking that I might be killing an innocent man!"

George Daugherty
ELKVIEW, WEST VIRGINIA

Not Your'n

A sweet young girl was jilted by her husband.
He left her and went his merry way.
With tear-filled eyes she wrote a final letter,
In which with broken heart she had this to say,
"I'm returning every present that you sent me,
I'm sending back each letter that you wrote,
Every sweet memento that we cherished,
Even the locket I wore around my throat.
Enclosed you'll find the mortgage to the house, dear.
In that I'm fair, you must admit is true.
I'm returning everything except the baby.
That's the one thing I didn't get from you!"

Composed by George Daugherty

Watch that Tree

There's this fellow over in Pulaski County, his wife died. Had an undertaker come for her. They carried the body out the front door on a big board, across the porch, down the steps. And as they went across the yard, headed for the hearse, that board bumped against a maple tree there in the yard, and that woman stirred. They began to work on her, and she revived.

That woman lived another ten years! Then she died again. And when the undertakers came for her this time, and started across the yard with her, her husband said, "Uh, boys, watch out for that tree there."

Dr. Jim W. Miller
BOWLING GREEN, KENTUCKY

Absence Makes the Heart ...

A couple was having some marital difficulty, and the man went to see a marriage counselor to see if he had some ideas.

The counselor said, "I'm a great believer in exercise. My advice is to walk at least ten miles a day."

About a week later the man called the counselor and he asked how things were going.

The man said, "Just fine, I took your advice. I've been walking ten miles a day, and now I'm a hundred miles from home!"

Rev. William Hamilton, Sr.
BEREA, KENTUCKY

Prolific

There was this other woman who had so many children, she ran out of names to call her husband.

Minnie Pearl
NASHVILLE, TENNESSEE

Envying the Expert

A woman who had been married and divorced four times was invited by a friend to go hear a professor from the local college speak on love and marriage. She listened intently. Afterwards, her friend asked her what she thought of the lecture.

"Well," she said, "I wish I knew as little about the subject as he did."

Elwood Cornett
BLACKEY, KENTUCKY

Reassuring

Young married couples often bring us pastors their problems. I'm thinking of the young bride who had not learned to cook before she married. One evening her husband came home and found his young wife crying. In an effort to comfort her, he asked what the problem was.

The wife replied, "The dog ate the biscuits."

The young husband sought to further comfort her by saying, "Never mind, honey. We'll get a new dog."

Rev. J. Harold Stephens
SHELBYVILLE, TENNESSEE

Overdrawn

Two women were gossiping, but one broke it off by saying, "I can't tell you any more. I've already told you more than I heard."

Loyal Jones

Burned Beans

This young couple got married, and she was kind of nervous cooking her first dinner. She fixed a big pot of beans and served her husband up a big plateful. He ate awhile, and then she asked him how the beans were.

"They're pretty good," he said, "but I believe they are a little bit burned."

Well, she said, "Them beans are not burned!" She got mad and they had a big fight over whether or not the beans were burned. They got so mad they didn't speak to each other for two weeks.

Finally, one day she came down and said, "I'm sorry for getting so mad. Let's make up."

He said, "You're right. It was silly of us to get so mad over those burned beans."

She said, "Them beans were not burned!"

Sam "Geezinslaw" Allred
SNOOK, TEXAS

Self-Sufficient

Two fellows were talking while they worked, but one of them didn't have much to say.

The other one asked him, "Did you wake up grouchy this morning?"

"No, I let her wake her own self up." he said.

Loyal Jones

On Suicide

Culbert Stamper, of Knott County, thought he was a ladies' man, a gay Lothario—until there appeared a young lady from the lowlands to teach in the local public school. It was in the days of the rubber-tired buggy, patent leather shoes, tight-fitting pants, and the mustache. Culbert suddenly took a liking to the new teacher, her face, dress, carriage, and all. He wanted to call on her, but every time he thought of it he could not muster up courage enough to ask her, for he saw at once that she was different from mountain girls. As long last he overcame his timidity, and bluntly asked the "furrin" lady for a date. Out of curiosity she accepted. Culbert called. They sat in the parlor. There was no conversation, for Culbert did not know how to begin or what to say. An hour passed.

Finally, to start conversation, the new teacher said to Culbert, "Mr. Stamper, what do you think of a man who commits suicide?"

Culbert lapsed into profound meditation, squirming in his chair, crossing one leg and then the other. Then he twisted both ends of his mustache, looked up, and replied sententiously,

"Well, Madam, I think he ought to be made to take the child and raise it."

The late Josiah H. Combs
PERRY COUNTY, KENTUCKY AND
FT. WORTH, TEXAS

Sizing Her Up

A friend of mine went into a lingerie shop to buy a brassiere for his wife. He didn't realize he had to know the size, but the friendly saleslady tried to help him out. "How about the size of a grapefruit?" she asked.

"No, smaller," he said.

"About like oranges?"

"No, smaller."

"Then, how about eggs?"

"Yeah, fried," said my friend.

Lonnie "Pap" Wilson
NASHVILLE, TENNESSEE

Fifty-Fifty

Marriage is a fifty-fifty proposition. The men tell us what to do, and we tell them where to go.

Minnie Pearl
NASHVILLE, TENNESSEE

Couldn't Think of a Word

There was this woman who talked so slow that before she could say she wasn't that kind of woman, she was.

Dr. John Fenn
BRANFORD, CONNECTICUT

Perspective

Two relatives were talking, and one asked, "How did that mean little Harry of yours get that knot on his head?"

The other one replied, "Your little angel Susie hit him with a brick."

> The late Raymond Layne
> BEREA, KENTUCKY

Changing World

Wife: "You used to tell me that I was all the world to you."
Husband: "Yeah, but my knowledge of geography was limited then."

> *Raymond Layne*

Shhh

This man called a friend's house, and their little daughter answered.
"Is your father there?" he asked.
"Yes," whispered the little girl.
"May I speak with him?"
"No, he's busy," she whispered again.
"May I speak with your mother?"
"No, she's busy."
"May I speak with your brother then?"
"No, he's busy too."
"What are they doing?"
"Looking for me," the little girl whispered.

> *Randy Travis*
> NASHVILLE, TENNESSEE

The Other Solution

A couple was celebrating their fiftieth wedding anniversary. A friend asked the wife if she had ever considered divorcing her husband.

She said, "No, we don't divorce in my family, but I've thought of killing him a few times."

> *Jessie Schneidewind*
> DEARBORN, MICHIGAN

Fairy Story

A woman went into a pet shop looking for a pet. She saw this frog that winked at her and made a kissing sound. She went on and looked at the puppies, kittens and parakeets, and then she went back to the frog. It winked at her and made a kissing sound again. She thought that was cute, and so she bought it.

Driving home, she took him out of his box and set him on the seat beside her. When she looked down, it again winked at her and made the kissing sound. She leaned over and kissed it, and lo, it turned into a handsome prince!

The woman turned into a motel!

Averill Kilbourne
BEREA, KENTUCKY

Not Always

A census taker went to a house and knocked. A woman came out, and he said, "How many children do you have, and what are their ages?"

She said, "Well, there are the twins, Sally and Holly, they're eighteen. And the twins Billie and Willie, they're sixteen. And the twins Charlie and Jenny, they're fourteen ... "

"Hold on," said the census taker. "Did you get twins every time?"

"No, there were hundreds of times we didn't get anything."

Ralph Emery
NASHVILLE, TENNESSEE

Serving Time

I saw this man and woman all dressed up having a nice dinner in this hotel, but he was crying.

She said, "Honey, why are you crying? This is our twenty-fifth wedding anniversary."

He said, "Do you remember when your father caught us hugging and kissing in the bushes, and he said if I didn't marry you

I'd spend the next twenty-five years in jail?"

She said, "Yes, I remember that, but why are you crying now?"

He said, "I'd be getting out today!"

Mel Tillis
BRANSON, MISSOURI

All Over

You pretty well know the honeymoon is over when you call home to say you'll be late for supper and your wife has already left a note that it is in the oven.

Loyal Jones

Priorities

My grandfather, John Payne, of Disputanta, Kentucky, told me this story:

A long time ago, I used to ride around Rockcastle County. One time, along about nightfall, I came to a poor-looking farm. I asked the farmer if he'd mind putting me up for the night. He agreed and apologized for being so poor, without more to offer.

At supper, I sat across from his wife, and she was one of the most beautiful women I have ever seen. He put a plate in front of each of us, cut each a meager piece of cornbread, and carefully measured out two spoonsful of beans on each place. He said they would have to save the rest for tomorrow.

After the plates were washed and put away, I settled down on the floor and went right to sleep. About 2:00 in the morning a sound woke me up, and the farmer's wife was sitting beside me.

I whispered and asked her if her husband slept soundly. In the firelight I could see her smile and nod her beautiful head.

"Good," I said. "Let's help ourselves to those beans."

Gregory Oliver
MANSFIELD, TEXAS

Bullish Bickering

A man and woman went to a cattle auction. They had three top bulls auctioned off that day. After the sale, the woman asked the auctioneer, "How many times a year would that third most expensive bull be active?" The auctioneer guessed about fifty times. The woman turned to her husband and said, "See?"

She asked, "How many times would that second bull be active?" He said maybe seventy-five times. She turned to her husband and said, "See?"

She asked how many times the highest priced bull would be active. He said maybe about a hundred times. She again turned to her husband even more forcefully and said, "See?"

The husband said to the auctioneer. "Would all of those times be with the same cow?" The auctioneer said of course not. The husband turned to his wife and said, "See?"

Jim Stafford
NASHVILLE, TENNESSEE

Practice Makes Painful

Smoky: "My wife and I have been married for fifteen years, and she's been throwing things at me ever since we got married."

Luke: "Why have you just now started complaining?"

Smoky: "Her aim's getting better."

The late Archie Campbell
NASHVILLE, TENNESSEE

Keeping Mum

Dennis Bailey, a friend of mine, finally had to admit that his hearing was bad. A doctor fitted him with a hearing aid and told him to come back in a couple of weeks for a check-up. When he went back, he was enthusiastic about how much his hearing had improved. He said he could sit in the living-room and hear everything that was said in the kitchen.

"Your family must be happy for you," said the doctor.

"I haven't told them yet," said Dennis. "I've already changed my will three times from what I've heard."

Jesse Butcher
KNOXVILLE, TENNESSEE

Not My Line

This woman asked her husband if he would fix a faulty light switch. He responded, "Do I look like Thomas Edison?"

A day or two later she asked him if he could move her telephone to a more convenient location. He said, "Do I look like Alexander Graham Bell?"

The next day he came home, and his wife pointed out that their neighbor had fixed the light switch and moved the phone.

"Did you pay him?" her husband asked.

"Yes, he said I could bake him a cake or go to bed with him."

"What flavor of cake did you bake?" he asked.

"Do I look like Betty Crocker?" she responded.

Hilda Woodie
BEREA, KENTUCKY

Progress

A farmer who lived a way back in the hills had a twenty-one-year-old son who'd never been to town. The old man figured it was time to learn the boy a thing or two about modern life. So they hitchhiked into the city. They marveled at the electric lights and the three- and four-story skyscrapers, and presently found themselves inside a large department store.

They looked over to one wall, and there was a big set of jaws with an arrow on top that went from one to four. Every now and then the jaws would open and close. The old man was really outside of his element and had no idea what the contraption was, but he didn't want to let on how ignorant he was. So he and the boy just stood there and watched.

About that time, up waddled an old fat woman. She pushed

the button, the jaws opened, she stepped in, and the jaws closed behind her. The arrow went from one to two to three to four, then back to three to two to one. They opened and out stepped a trim young woman about twenty-five. She pranced past the two men with a smile.

As soon as she was out of sight, the old man took off his hat, hit his son over the head with it, and said, "Hale far, boy! Time's wastin'! We got to go git Maw and run her through that thang!"

Sam Venable
KNOXVILLE, TENNESSEE

The Cat on the Roof

There were two brothers, Albert and Buford, who lived on a farm with their mom. Albert had a neutered tomcat named Mitty-Kitty. He'd been named Mittens as a baby, but then they just called him Mitty-Kitty because they thought he was cute, and the name sort of stuck.

Buford, Mom, and Mitty-Kitty ran the farm, but Albert went off to the University of Kentucky and got a B.S. degree so he wouldn't have to work. He was on the road a lot, taking orders for fertilizer and other agricultural chemicals.

Albert would call back often to check on Mitty-Kitty, because he loved that cat. Well, anyway, one day he called back and Buford answered the phone, and he said, "Albert, Mitty-Kitty is dead. A car hit him, smashed him flat as a pancake, and drove off. We don't know where the car went or who was driving it."

Albert was pretty torn up about it. He sobbed a minute and then he said, "Buford, it's bad enough that Mitty-Kitty is dead, but at least you could have broken it to me gently, not just told me all at once, just like that! What you should have done, you should have told me that Mitty-Kitty was up on the roof and you couldn't get him down. Then the next time I called, you could've said, 'We finally got him down, but it got to raining and we think he's got pneumonia. He's not looking good.' And then, after a few calls like this, you could have let me know that he'd gone on to be with the Lord."

Buford said, "Well, Albert, I apologize. I know how much you loved Mitty-Kitty, and I'm sorry."

Albert said, "Well, I understand. You never cared much for him yourself, but I understand your position. By the way, how's Mom?"

Buford said, "She's up on the roof, and we can't get her down ..."

Albert Wilson
FRANKFORT, KENTUCKY

No Family Resemblance, He Claimed

Monford, a sixty-six-year-old mountain man, had worked at Clyde's Cadillac in Charleston, West Virginia, for twenty-one years and never missed a day. But today he walked into the boss's office looking worried. Clyde asked him what was wrong.

"Well, Boss, I got a problematical situation," he said. "I got to go see the judge on account o' this girl claiming I got her in a family way. She's hitting me with a paternity suit. I'm gonna need the day off."

Naturally the boss let him go.

A few days later Monford came back from test driving a car with a customer when he ran into Clyde, who asked him, "How did your day in court go, Monford?"

"Not good, sir. Not good."

"What happened?"

"Well sir," Monford answered, "there she sat ... holding that baby in her arms. And I said to the judge, I said, your honor ... you look at that baby and you look at me. That baby don't look *nothing* like me."

"So, what'd the judge say?"

"The judge said, 'You keep feeding him till he does.' "

Chet Atkins, C.G.P.
NASHVILLE, TENNESSEE

Dangerous Secret

This woman, she secretly went out and bought a lottery ticket and won twenty million, but her husband had a bad heart and she was afraid to tell him because she was afraid he'd keel right over. She went to her pastor and told him about the situation. The pastor said, "Let me take him out to lunch and I'll see if I can let him know subtly."

So, they went to lunch and the preacher said after a while, "I notice that people have been winning the lottery a lot."

The lady's husband said, "Yes, I guess so."

The preacher said, "What would you do if you should win the lottery? Say you won twenty million dollars, what would you do with it?" He said, "Well, first off, I'd give half of it to the church."

When he heard that, the *preacher* had a heart attack!

Lee Morris
BEREA, KENTUCKY

The Farmer's Three Daughters

There was a farmer who had three daughters and he wasn't doing too well at getting them married off, so he offered a reward to anyone who would take any one of them.

He had five hundred dollars on one, and fifty dollars on another, but the pretty one didn't have a price on her.

A prospect came by, went in to see the daughters, and asked the farmer how he arrived at his price scheduling.

The farmer said, "Well, the first daughter is a little bit bow-legged. The second daughter is a little bit knock-kneed."

The man asked about the one who didn't have a price on her, the young pretty one.

The father said, "Well, that one ... she's just a little bit pregnant."

Glen Baker
FAIRMONT, WEST VIRGINIA

Voluntary Vacation

A man in the coal business was bragging about his vacation, saying, "I took my wife to the West Indies."

"Jamaica?" a friend asked.

"No, she wanted to go."

Loyal Jones

Just Right Pie

Hiram Holbrook and several other farmers were exchanging work to strip tobacco. One day when Hiram's neighbors were at his house, his wife was cooking and baking for the big noon dinner. One of the pies was slightly burned. Believing that nothing but the best should be served the neighbors, she kept this pie out for supper that night. After Hiram ate most of it, she asked, "How was that pie, Hiram?"

"Just right." he said. "If it had been burned any more, I couldn't have eaten it, and if it had been burned less I wouldn't have got it. So, it was just right."

Juanita Slater
WEST VIRGINIA
(NOW LIVING IN CINCINNATI)

LAWYERS AND POLITICIANS:

Better Side-Steppers than Two-Steppers

Bible, Bucks, or Booze?

A couple heard that they could ascertain which direction their infant son would go by putting certain objects in front of him to see which interested him most. So they put the Bible, a bottle of whiskey, and a twenty-dollar bill in front of him. The infant grabbed all three.

"Oh, Lord, he's going to be a politician," the father said.

Norman Parsons
WHITLEY CITY, KENTUCKY

A Comic Custody Case

Judges make mistakes, I can tell you that. I was a trial court judge for many years, but I still like the story about the lady who was very happy about the divorce decree the judge had entered, although he'd made a mistake. She put it in the form of a verse and wrote:

Ain't life grand!
I just got a divorce from my old man!
I laughed and laughed at the judge's decision,
He gave *him* the kids, and they ain't even *his'n!*

Judge Ray Corns
LOUISVILLE, KENTUCKY

Bound to the Truth

The country musician agreed with his attorney in a divorce case that he might be a little bit conceited but that he had every right to be.

The attorney asked, "How could you stand up there in court and say that you are the greatest living guitar picker?"

The musician said, "I was under oath, you'll remember, and I didn't want to commit perjury."

Loyal Jones

Suited for the Job

A fellow applied for the job as press spokesman for the state legislature. He went for an interview. The interviewer said, "Your application is full of exaggeration, distortion, and lies. Can you come to work Monday?"

Loyal Jones

Observation

Grandpa Jones and Mike Snider were guests of Ralph Emery on "Nashville Now," discussing taxes.

Mike: "The Internal Revenue Service says that we work four months out of the year for the government."

Grandpa: "That's more than government employees work for the government."

Grandpa Jones
NASHVILLE, TENNESSEE

Mike Snider
GLEASON, TENNESSEE

Saddle Up

A federal agency with a young representative from New York had a pig chain going among farmers in a mountain county in Tennessee. Six farmers were called together by the young fellow to talk pigs. He told the farmers they had plenty of feed because of the fine grass on their farms. Asked if they could get some grain included, the youngster told them there had been no provision for grain.

One of the farmers then asked the New Yorker if it would be possible to buy saddles for the older pigs so that the children could ride them the mile and a half down the creek to meet the school bus.

"How much would these saddles cost?" asked the New Yorker.

"I think I can get them for about $8.00 a piece," the farmer replied.

The New Yorker studied a moment and then replied, "I think that could be arranged."

Turning to his neighbor, the farmer remarked, "I reckon I just arranged for the corn."

Fred Burkhard
LIBERTY, KENTUCKY

The Sane Politician

A candidate for political office had been in the mental hospital, and his opponent brought it up in a debate.

He pulled forth a certificate of release from the hospital and said, "I'm the only candidate who can produce a valid certificate of sanity."

The late Honorable Brooks Hays
LITTLE ROCK, ARKANSAS

Baldfaced

Another candidate for office was accused by his opponent of being illiterate.

He heatedly responded, "That's a damned lie. My pappy and mammy was married six months before I was born."

Loyal Jones

Sentence Fragment

When someone introduced a certain senator as "North Carolina's favorite son," a fellow standing nearby said, "That ain't a complete sentence."

Loyal Jones

Too Plain

Congressman Davy Crockett of Tennessee, after listening to a speech by Senator Daniel Webster was said to have commented, "I've heard you are a great man. I don't believe it. I understood every word of your speech."

Billy Edd Wheeler

Plenty Good Enough

I stopped in the court house square of a small eastern Kentucky town to visit with an old lady who was sitting on a bench there. The court house was brand new, and I asked her what she thought of it.

She said, "Well, the old one was plenty good enough for what went on there."

The late Dr. Raymond B. Drukker
BEREA, KENTUCKY

Short Supply

A country fellow went to town for the first time. He walked around looking into store windows, impressed with the range of goods. He wandered into the court house and opened a door where the county judge and county attorney were conferring.

"What are you fellers selling?" he said.

"Blockheads," said the irritated judge.

"Well," said the fellow, "business must be good since you only got two left."

Ralph Miner
JONESVILLE, VIRGINIA

Touchy Ground

The counsels in a case were questioning jurors to empanel a jury. The first person, a woman, was asked by the prosecuting attorney if she knew the counsel for the defense.

"I sure do," she said. "He's a notorious womanizer."

The defense counsel rose and said, "Do you know the prosecuting attorney?"

"I sure do," she said. "He passes bad checks."

After they had dismissed the woman from service, the judge asked the attorneys to approach the bench and said, "It's all right for you to ask any questions you want to about attorneys in this case, but don't you dare ask any questions about the judge."

Judge William Jennings
RICHMOND, KENTUCKY

Missing Influence

There was a man who had named his son after a judge. He and the judge met on the street years later and the judge asked how the son was doing.

The man said, "Well, just after he was born I got sent to the federal pen for moonshining, and I'd no more than got home before Jim Sims acted up, and I had to kill him. They sent me to the state pen that time. That boy growed up out of my influence, and he didn't turn out too good."

The late Honorable Brooks Hays
LITTLE ROCK, ARKANSAS

Not Robert's Rules

A man was being tried for murder, for shooting a man at a public meeting. He was asked by the prosecuting attorney why he shot him.

"Well, he made a motion that was out of order."

"You mean you shot him in cold blood for making a motion?"

"Yeah, he made a motion toward his pocket."

Brooks Hays

Good Learner

Former Sheriff Jesse James Bailey, of Madison County, North Carolina, told me about the last public hanging in the county, about 1920 or 1921. They brought the guy out and asked, "Do you have anything to say to these good people of Madison County before we hang you?"

He stepped forward and said, "I jist want you'ns to know that this shore is going to be a lesson to me!"

Billy Edd Wheeler

Persuasive

There was an eloquent lawyer in Henry County, Kentucky, who took on the case of a man who was accused of stealing a safe. The evidence, wholly circumstantial, was presented by the attorney for the prosecution, and the defense lawyer made a mighty argument for his client's innocence. The jury retired, and while they were waiting the lawyer said to his client,

"Now, I never asked you straight out if you stole that safe. Now that the arguments are made and the jury sequestered and since this won't influence the trial one way or another, did you steal that safe?"

The defendant thought and scratched his head, "Well, before you made that speech, I was pretty sure I stole that safe, but now I'm just not sure at all."

Wendell Berry
PORT ROYAL, KENTUCKY

What About the Hat?

A man was accused of a crime, and the main evidence was a hat found at the scene of the crime, said to belong to the defendant. There was much argument pro and con, but the jury was not convinced that the hat belonged to the defendant, and they found him innocent. While the prosecutor was packing up he noticed the former defendant hanging around and inquired what he wanted.

"Well," he said, "I just wondered if I could have my hat."

Stuart Victor
FRANKFORT, KENTUCKY

Inflamed

When I was Circuit Judge, I never realized how many people would come in and ask two questions: "Can you marry us?" and "How much do you charge?" I'd say, "Yes" and "Nothing." I never had anyone who had filled out the marriage application, so it would take a few minutes to answer all of the questions and fill out the form with appropriate answers.

One day, this couple from Peoria, Illinois, came in—about forty years old, looked like intelligent people, neatly dressed, her hair looking like an explosion in a mattress factory. I was going down the list, asking her these questions, and I asked her, "Have you been married previously?"

"Yes, once," she said.

The next question, "Was it terminated by death or divorce?"

She said, "Death." While I was writing this down, she kept on talking. She seemed apprehensive. She said, "He died from one of them cerebral hemorrhoids!"

Now, I've been in the state capital for thirty-three years, and that suddenly opened my eyes. I realized what disease was affecting a lot of people I knew in high places. That moved the science of pathology several hundred light years forward!

Judge Ray Corns
FRANKFORT, KENTUCKY

In Absentia

St. Peter was out inspecting the big wall that separated

Heaven from Hell. Now, he had complained to Lucifer several times about his not keeping up his side of the wall. It was in worse shape, and he called Lucifer up to the wall and said, "If you don't fix your side of the wall and maintain it, I'm going to sue you."

Lucifer said, "Fine, where are you going to get your lawyers?"

Billy Edd Wheeler

Ineligible

A fellow decided to run for office, and he went out campaigning. He met up with a man he knew and asked him to vote for him.

"I wouldn't vote for you if you were St. Peter," the man replied. The would-be politician retorted. "I know that. You wouldn't be in my precinct."

Rev. William Hamilton, Sr.
BEREA, KENTUCKY

The Pilot and the Woodchopper

Ohio passed a law prohibiting any more Kentuckians from moving to Ohio, but someone pointed out that Ohio got a lot of doctors, lawyers, nurses, teachers and such from Kentucky. So, they amended the law to allow skilled people to enter. Police would stop people at the state line and question them.

A fellow drove up and stopped. They asked, "What do you do?"

"I'm a pilot," he said, and they let him go in.

The fellow just behind him drove up and they asked him the same question. "I'm a wood-chopper," he said.

"You can't come in," the policeman said. "We already have more wood-choppers than we need."

"But you let my cousin in that red pick-up in," the man said.

"Yes, but he is a pilot."

"Well, he can't pile it if I don't chop it," he said.

Jim Hinsdale
WARSAW, KENTUCKY

Over-Overruling

Judge Calhoun was the first county judge of Knott County, in the 1880s. He was hearing a case, and made a decision contrary to all law and precedent.

One of the lawyers protested vigorously, "Why, your Honor, when you rule that way you are doing something contrary to the statute."

"In that case," answered his Honor, "I'm overruling the statute."

Dr. Josiah H. Combs
PERRY COUNTY, KENTUCKY
AND FORT WORTH, TEXAS

Tact

Lawyer Stowers of Pikeville was a born diplomat and a suave gentleman. One day a lady, accompanied by a poodle dog, met him on the street, and they began to chat. In a little while the dog walked over and began to smell Stowers's legs, then started to raise a hind leg to perform a very common canine function. Stowers jumped back out of the way.

"Oh, Mr. Stowers, I'm so sorry."

"Never mind, I thought he was going to kick me."

Josiah H. Combs

Patient Politician

The late Governor Bert T. Combs, who was from the mountains of eastern Kentucky, told this story on himself. He said that while he was governor, there was a tour bus that took visitors around the capital city, showing them the sights. He decided to go incognito on the tour, so he went down to board the bus. There was a group of patients from Eastern State Hospital, the mental hospital, and he went in and sat down among them.

The social worker in charge thought he'd better count his patients to make sure they all got aboard, so he started, "One, two, three, four, five, six ... , wait a minute, who are you?"

Governor Combs said, "I am Bert T. Combs, Governor of Kentucky."

The social worker said, "Seven, eight, nine ... "

John Ed McConnell
FRANKFORT, KENTUCKY

Uncharitable Chairman

Once when Emerson "Doc" Beauchamps was running for one of his numerous offices in the primary of a certain Kentucky county, the Democratic chairman thought it wouldn't be good for the popular "Doc" to completely overwhelm his opponent, so he told "Doc" to hang back a little in his speeches, and "let him have about nine votes."

Came election day, and "Doc" got every Democratic vote that was cast. The chairman said to him, "I thought I told you to hold back and give him about nine votes."

"Doc" said, "Oh, I thought you said, 'Nary'n.' "

The Honorable Wendell Butler
FRANKFORT, KENTUCKY

Liberalized

When Louie B. Nunn was the Republican governor of Kentucky, his wife Beulah spent considerable time getting the state to take over the estate of Cassius Marcellus Clay, Minister to Russia under Abraham Lincoln, and in getting White Hall, Clay's residence, restored. One day Governor and Mrs. Nunn called on Mrs. Esther Bennett, granddaughter of Clay, who shared some family lore.

Apparently the Clay family had been embarrassed when, during a party at White Hall after Clay had returned from Russia, the Russian ambassador arrived and presented a small boy, the result of Clay's affair with a Russian ballerina. Clay, of course, was married, but his wife had not accompanied him to Russia.

When Mrs. Nunn heard the story, she was very sympathetic

to Mrs. Bennett and said she could understand the stress and strain Mr. Clay had been through in far-off Russia without the comfort of his wife and family, the long Russian winters, the long nights, and so forth. The Governor, a conservative, listened in some surprise at his wife's liberal attitude.

On their drive back to Frankfort, Mrs. Nunn asked her husband if he had given thought to what he would like to do after his term of office was over.

He said, "Well, you know, I've been thinking about applying for the ambassadorship to Russia!"

Dr. James C. Murphy
RICHMOND, KENTUCKY

Don't Try to Fool Me

A not-too-bright deputy sheriff caught a tourist driving too fast and pulled him over. He walked up and asked, "Where are you from?"

"Chicago." the man replied.

"Don't pull that stuff on me," said the deputy, "your license says Illinois."

Dr. Buck Henson
WISE, VIRGINIA

Neither One

A judge in Paintsville, Kentucky, was calling up a case, and he said, "Will the defendant please rise."

A fellow rose and said, "The defendant is sick today. I'm his brother, and I'm here to represent him."

The judge asked, "What are your qualifications for representing him? Are you a lawyer?"

The fellow said, "No, I ain't," and started to leave.

The judge called after him, "What's your brother sick of?"

The fellow turned around and said, "I ain't no doctor either," and went on out.

Rod Bussey
BEREA, KENTUCKY

Contacts

There is the story about the man whose driver's license required that he wear glasses when driving. He was stopped by a county sheriff and told, "Boy, you're going to jail for driving without glasses."

He replied, "But Sheriff, I have contacts."

And the sheriff said, "I don't care who you know, boy. You're going to jail."

Dr. John C. Wolff, Jr.
LEXINGTON, KENTUCKY

Zebulon Vance and the Beans

Zebulon B. Vance, Civil War officer, North Carolina's wartime governor and later United States senator, was from Buncombe County in the Old North State. He possessed an abundance of mountain wit and many stories are told about him. The following one is from the late Bascom Lamar Lunsford, musician, festival promoter, song and story collector, and quite a wit himself.

It's said that when Zebulon B. Vance used to go around on his political campaigns, he'd tell his wife to fix him up a couple of little packages of beans. He'd spend the night at some place, and, of course, they would talk late into the night. Before he left, he'd say, "I about forgot. My wife told me to tell you (speaking to the lady of the house) that she wanted you to have some of her seed beans, that they are good. And she said you always have such good beans, she wanted you to send her some of your seed beans, if you would."

And she'd say, "Why, yes, I'll do that. I'll fix up some." So she would fix up some other packages and tie them up. Before he'd leave, she'd say, "Here are the beans you can give your wife. Tell her, now, this is a bunch bean, and that this is a running bean."

"All right," he thanked her very much, and he'd go on to another valley and spend the night in the home of some farmer who had a lot of renters and was close to people whom he could influence in the election. But before he'd leave he would say, "Well, Mrs. Ramsey (or Mrs. Rector, or Mrs. whoever it might be), my wife wanted some of your seed beans and she wants to know if you would be willing to send her a few. She sent some with me, if I can find them. Yes, here they are, and she wants you to have these seed beans, and she wants some of yours. You have always had such good beans, and those you had yesterday for dinner, I think, are the best I ever tasted."

So the good lady would go on and fix up a couple packages of beans and say, "Now, this one is a butter bean and this one is the Lazy Wife bean."

The packages of beans would go from one to the other, and maybe the great governor never did get back home with any of the beans he had collected. But he always got votes.

The late Bascom Lamar Lunsford
LEICESTER, NORTH CAROLINA

FDR and Brooks Hays

The following story was related by Brooks Hays, then Congressman from the 5th District of Arkansas, in a letter to Congressman Franklin D. Roosevelt, Jr. of New York dated January 9, 1951. His purpose was to tell the younger Roosevelt about a trip he took with FDR to Arkansas and Texas in 1936 for Centennial celebrations in those states. The President gave a dinner for various politicians and government officials one evening, and the talk turned to politics, among other things.

The President made the point that in political campaigns it is very difficult to popularize the tax reform program because it is always too technical for the average voter, and for confirmation he turned to me as an old campaigner and said, "Hasn't that been your experience?" I am not sure that he knew that I had been defeated twice for governor but since he set the stage for me I told him one of my stories.

I said, "Mr. President, I have a perfect illustration, I believe, of that point. In 1928 I was a candidate for Governor of Arkansas and was probably the first candidate in the State's history to advocate an income tax. At Big Flat, in Baxter County, forty miles from the railroad, deep in the Ozark woods, I was talking to seventy-five voters about my program. It must have been rather technical, because right in the middle of my dissertation a blacksmith, leaning against his shop, said, 'Hold on—can I ask you a question?' And when I told him I would be glad to answer him he said, 'That talk about taxes is all right, I reckon, but what we folks here at Big Flat want to know is, how do you stand on evolution?'"

Your father laughed heartily and the conversation was about to turn to another subject when he said, "What did you tell that fellow?" I said, "Mr. President, I think I can sum it up best by saying that after I was gone, one of my listeners was heard to comment, 'You know, if that fellow is as good a two-stepper as he is a side-stepper, he is popular at the Little Rock dances.' "

State Capitol Punishment

Kentucky teacher to kid: "Why do you not believe in capital punishment?"

Kid: "I don't want to live in Frankfort!"

Charlie Tribble
CYNTHIANA, KENTUCKY

The Judge Travels First Class

My favorite story about judges concerns one in New York, having breakfast alone in a local restaurant. A stranger came in and sat down at the same table, and they saw a big ad in that day's edition of *The New York Times*. The ad read: "Caribbean Cruise—Miami and Return—Total cost fifty dollars." The stranger said, "Boy, that's too good to be true!" The New York judge said, "Sounds like it, but why don't we jet down there today and check this thing out?"

So, they caught the next flight to Miami and went out to the docks, and paid the man their money. He hit them on the head and knocked them out, tied them on a log and pushed them out to sea. Half-hour later, the stranger came to and asked the judge, "I wonder, do they serve drinks on this cruise?" The judge said, "They didn't last year."

Judge Ray Corns
LOUISVILLE, KENTUCKY

Judicious Change of Mind

A woman who was summoned to serve on jury duty said to the judge, "I can't serve, your Honor, I don't believe in capital punishment."

He said, "Well, this is not a capital case, it's a civil matter. This man stole $10,000 and ran off to spend it on another woman."

She said, "I'll serve, your Honor. I could be wrong about capital punishment."

The late Honorable Brooks Hayes
LITTLE ROCK, ARKANSAS

Old Bill Jones

Everybody seemed to know Old Bill Jones. When the President came through town in a motorcade, he called out to Old Bill as he went by. When Marilyn Monroe came to town, she asked about Old Bill Jones. He got letters from all sorts of important people.

Well, this fellow knew about Old Bill Jones and wondered how he got so famous, looked him up and said, "You seem to know everybody, but I bet you don't know the Pope." Old Bill said he did and that he was soon going to see him in Rome. The man said he'd like to go along because he didn't believe Old Bill knew the Pope.

So they went to Rome, and Old Bill said he'd go in and see the Pope and then he'd come out on the balcony with him and that the fellow could see for himself. So this fellow went out there and got in this big crowd. Pretty soon Old Bill Jones came out with several cardinals and a man in white. The fellow asked somebody next to him, "Is that the Pope?"

The man said, "I don't know, but that's Old Bill Jones."

The late Gutherie T. Meade
FRANKFORT, KENTUCKY

THE SPORTING LIFE:

Conning the Warden
and Other Exaggerations

Heavy Duty

My brother is a big hunter and sportsman. I get tired of his tales about hunting in the winter—doves, quail, turkeys, deer, bear—and then about fishing in the spring and summer. I heard all his stories about his big fish, bigger than anybody else caught. I found out the real story one day. These neighbors of my brother's had a baby, and they brought it over to weigh it on my brother's fish scales. That five-day-old baby weighed thirty-seven pounds!

Marc Pruett
ASHEVILLE, NORTH CAROLINA

Big Bait

My dad-in-law and I were fishing down on Lake Wiley one evening, and we knew about this old bass—ten or twelve pounds— that hung around this stump. We'd thrown the whole tackle box at him and never had any luck. We cast for him, but didn't get a rise out of him. We threw rubber frogs and anything we thought he might like, but we got no response. It was a losing proposition, so we went back to fishing for crappie.

A little while later we saw this squirrel come be-bopping out of the woods, bouncing up and down the bank. There was a big acorn on the stump where the bass hung out, and it must have looked tempting to him. He backed up, took a run, jumped onto that stump, and ate that acorn and watched us fish a little bit. He was all set to jump back onto the bank when that big bass came up out of the water—swoosh—and swallowed him whole!

"Did you see that?" my dad-in-law asked.

"No, I didn't," I said, "because that was a lie!"

We finally decided it was true, but since we knew that bass wouldn't strike anything now, we started fishing for crappie again. We fished for a while, and then we heard a commotion at the stump again.

"Did you see that?"

"No, what?"

"That bass just put another acorn on that stump!"

> Jim Hinsdale
> WARSAW, KENTUCKY

Checkin' for Licenses

This one is about an old friend, Jess Butcher, who is a retired game warden from Union County, Tennessee. Jess was the game warden, and the biggest crime he was asked to investigate was folks who didn't have that one-dollar fishing license. It was Jess's sworn duty to find them and fine them.

Well, he was going up the lake one day, in that big old boat the state gave him, puttering along, and he passed the mouth of a cove, saw three old boys up there hunkering down with fishing rods and lines thrown out into the lake. Jess just acted like he didn't see them, just went right on across the mouth of the cove. Jess said, "I knowed them boys and I knowed they didn't have no licenses. I knowed if I went right in there, they'd run like quail." So Jess was going to outsmart them. He went on up the lake a half-mile, pulled into the bank, climbed the ridge, got to the very top, came down the hollow and went from tree to tree, got down to the last fifty yards, crawled on his belly like a snake, and stepped out amongst the boys and said, "Boys, I'm with the fish and game department, and I need to see your-all's licenses."

They all jumped up and looked at each other and at him, and one of them took off running. Jess done what anybody would do, he chased him. Right back up the mountain they went, and that old boy would nearly let Jess catch him, and then he'd turn on the speed and off he'd go. He led Jess out nearly to where he started to get them fellers, and finally Jess gave a really big leap and tackled him.

They both stood up, and Jess said, "Son, I need to see your fishing license." The old boy reached into his overall bib pocket and pulled out a billfold and opened it up and pulled out his license and said, "Well, right here it is!"

Jess looked at him kind of crazy-like and said, "Son, if you had this license all the time, how come you run me up that hill?"

The old boy said, "Cause my brothers down yonder, they didn't have nary'n."

Any time after that, Jess said that if anybody started to run, he let him go and jumped the others!

> *Sam Venable*
> KNOXVILLE, TENNESSEE

Strike

The ball was so fast the batter didn't see it at all. The umpire called a strike.

"Did you see that ball?" the batter asked the umpire.

"Yes, I did, and it was a strike."

"Well," the batter said, "it sounded a little high to me."

> *The Honorable Brooks Hays*
> LITTLE ROCK, ARKANSAS

Substitute

Our baseball coach cut a senior who had played for three previous years for infraction of rules. The boy arrived at practice to plead his case, to no avail.

"You'll be seeing my dad," the boy threatened.

"Can he play third?" the coach asked.

> *Jim Hinsdale*
> WARSAW, KENTUCKY

Wait 'Til I See

Once I was teaching a swimming class at Berea College, and on the first day I asked the students to dive into the water. One fellow started floundering around, and I asked him, "Can't you swim?"

He said, "Well, I don't know. I never tried it before."

Dr. Oscar Gunkler
BEREA, KENTUCKY

Supportive Fans

The academic standing of the leading scorer on the University basketball team had come into question. The academic folks thought they'd better test him. The coaches, thinking to intimidate the academics, suggested that he be tested in front of the fans at half-time at a big game.

So they proceeded to examine the player. The first question was, "What is six times six, divided by two."

The player thought a minute and then said, "Eighteen."

A great roar came from the fans, "Give him another chance!"

Dan Robinson
CORBIN, KENTUCKY

I Saw It

A fellow who wore glasses and couldn't see too well was an avid hunter. One day he invited his girlfriend to go hunting with him. They walked along a woodland trail for a while.

Suddenly she asked, "Did you see that?"

He said, "No, what was it?"

She said, "A squirrel just ran across the trail in front of us." It bothered him, but they went on.

"Did you see that?" she asked. Again he said he didn't, and she said it was a rabbit. They went on with him feeling pretty bad.

"Didn't you see that?" she asked, and then went on to explain that a deer had crossed the trail a hundred yards ahead. By this time the fellow was pretty upset with himself and his girlfriend.

So when she again said, "Did you see that?" he said quickly, "Yes, I did."

She said, "Well, then, why did you step in it?"

Dr. John B. Stephenson
BEREA, KENTUCKY

Let's Fish

A game warden watched a fellow bring in boatload after boatload of fish from the local lake. He inquired about his success, and he was invited to go fishing with him the next morning.

The game warden appeared with full tackle and rods. The man rowed to the middle of the lake, reached under the seat and got a stick of dynamite, lighted it, and threw it into the water. The blast brought up a great number of fish.

Before the game warden could recover from his surprise, the man again reached under his seat, took another stick, lighted it and handed it to the warden. The game warden said, "I'm an officer of the law and I can't do this!"

The man said, "Are we going to talk or are we going to fish?"

Dr. John C. Wolff, Jr.
LEXINGTON, KENTUCKY

Wrong Direction

A hunter was going through the woods when he came upon two other hunters pulling a slain deer along by his tail. He said, "Why don't you pull him by his antlers. It would be easier."

One of them said, "Well we were doing that, but we kept getting farther from the truck."

Loyal Jones

First Timer

A man hit his first golf ball and made a hole in one. He threw his club down and said, "I quit. There's not much to this game."

Billy Wilson
BOBTOWN, KENTUCKY

Conning the Warden

This fellow went into the barber shop and started bragging about how he had hunted and fished for years without a license, that he was too slick for the game warden to catch him. The game warden's cousin was in the shop and went straight and told the warden.

He vowed to catch the fellow, waited a week, went up there behind his house before daylight. He saw the light go on, saw the smoke coming from the cookstove. Finally the fellow came out on the back porch with a cup of coffee, looked up in the woods and said, "John, I guess you're cold. Come in and have a cup of coffee." So he did.

The game warden waited about two weeks and went back up there behind the fellow's house. The same thing happened again: the fellow got up, started a fire, brewed up some coffee, came out on the porch with a cup, and called to the game warden to come in and have some.

The game warden was puzzled and asked, "How did you know I was out there?"

"I didn't," the fellow said, "I come out and say that every morning."

Ben Davis
BEREA, KENTUCKY

Too Hot to Trot

Three men from my home county of Lewis went on a fox hunt, and one of them had what you call an artificial limb. A wooden leg, if you please. Well, the first thing you do while you're waiting for the dogs to hit that trail and make that music, as they call it, you build up a big brush fire. They did that, but no music! Then, they drank some coffee, and some other "stuff" for which Kentucky is well noted. Still no music. So, they decided they'd lie down and take a rest. They all went to sleep.

During the course of his slumber, the man with the wooden leg got too close to the blaze, caught his leg on fire, and burned it off, unknown to him. About the time black darkness had fallen, the dogs suddenly hit a red-hot trail and started making that

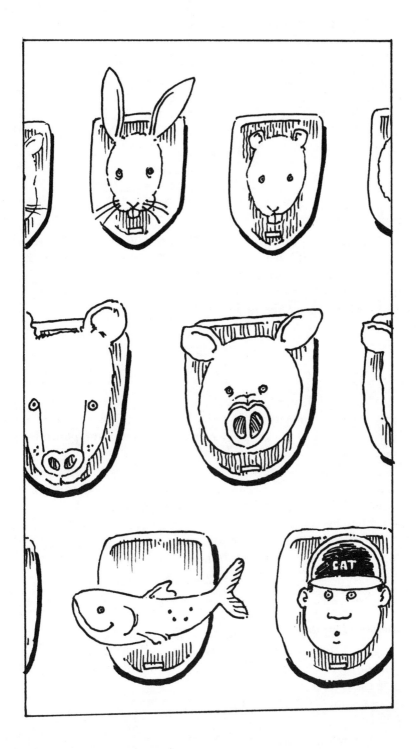

music up and down the valley and across the hills.

As is the custom, the men jumped up in the darkness and ran toward the dogs, with this man who just lost his leg (but didn't know it) leading the group. After they had run about two hundred feet, he turned to his two friends and yelled, "Watch out! After every other step, there's a great big hole!"

Judge Ray Corns
LOUISVILLE, KENTUCKY

In This Together

I was driving down I-75 this afternoon with a friend named Charlie, and traffic was pretty heavy. I was moving along pretty keen when Charlie said, "You damn fool, you're doing eighty miles per hour!"

I looked over at him and said, "Well, so are you."

Phil Davis
ALEXANDRIA, INDIANA

Fast and Slow

There was this kid, we'll call him Sammy Smith, who went to a high school in Appalachia. He was a whiz at football, but dumb as a sack of rocks. They tutored him day and night to keep him eligible.

A few years ago he was the running back who gained more than two hundred yards in the Super Bowl. I was talking to Sammy's high school coach, and mentioned what a star Sammy Smith had become.

The coach got a faraway look in his eyes, sighed deeply and said, "That kid could do anything with a football except sign it."

Chinquapin Jones
GRAVEL SWITCH, KENTUCKY

Common Hobbies

This golfer proposed to a woman and she accepted. So he went on to tell her how devoted he was to golf, that he would be gone most weekends, and so on.

She said, "Well, that's all right. I'm a hooker."

He said, "Don't worry about it. Just keep your head down and your left arm straight."

Loyal Jones

How To Catch A Rabbit

The way you catch a rabbit is to hide in the briar patch and make a noise like a carrot.

Chinquapin Jones
GRAVEL SWITCH, KENTUCKY

How To Catch A Polar Bear

The way to catch a polar bear is this: First you cut a hole in the ice and spread peas all around the edge of the hole. Then when the bear leans over to take a pea, you kick him in the ice hole.

Lee Turner
JACKSONVILLE, FLORIDA

Heavyweight Trophy Hunters

Two West Virginia boys started going to Canada on hunting trips. They got one of those planes that had those things on the bottom that could land out on a lake. The pilot would drop them in and come back a week later to pick them up.

A week went by once and when the pilot came back he found the West Virginians had bagged a large moose, and they were dead set on flying him out with them. But the pilot said, "Now look, boys, this plane is a four-seater and that moose weighs a good thousand pounds. With all three of us in that plane, plus the moose, we'll never get airborne. We're just too heavy a load."

They begged and pleaded but the pilot said no. Finally they called him a chicken and told him that last year they had a moose that same size, and that pilot managed to take off with them. So the pilot gave in, against his better judgment, and they loaded the moose into the plane.

The plane skimmed across the lake and lifted into the air just enough to crash into a hillside. About 48 hours later they came to. One looked at the other and said, "Clem, can you tell where we're at?"

Clem said, "Well Zeke, I think we're about one hundred yards farther than we got last year."

Ivan Tribe
MCARTHUR, OHIO

A Lesson In Field Dressing

Those two West Virginia boys decided not to go to Canada one year, opting to hunt closer to home. They headed for the Chief Cornstalk Public Hunting and Wildlife Area near Point Pleasant, hunting along the lower Kanawha River country. But they never did see a deer.

So one said to the other, "I tell you what, you stay here with the guns and I'll go back into that heavy brush back there. When I scare out a deer, you shoot it."

He watched his buddy disappear and stood there an hour with his finger on the trigger. It was cold. He was tense. After another hour his trigger finger was getting pretty itchy when, all of a sudden, he hears a lot of rustling noise in the brush. He pulls the trigger, fires, and rushes into the brush. "Oh my gosh," he screams, "I shot my buddy!"

He rushes the wounded man to the hospital's emergency room and paces the floor while the doctors operate. After an hour and a half a doctor comes out with a sad look on his face. "Well, Doc," he says, "is my buddy going to make it?"

"No," the doctor replies, "no, he's not. But he would have if you hadn't skinned him and gutted him!"

Ivan Tribe

Truthful's Tragic Fish Tale

There was a blacksmith shop in Kentucky at the Forks of Elkhorn where a lot of tale tellers hung out, the most eloquent of which was a man named Truthful Dawkins. Truthful was a great fisherman who came to be known as a jake-legged biologist.

One day he came to the blacksmith shop and told about a fish that followed him home from Elkhorn Creek. They didn't believe him, at first, but they thought it was funny so they asked him how it happened.

"I was crossing Elkhorn Creek on the swinging bridge," he said, "when I saw this seven or eight pound bass at the edge of the water being captured by a snake. The bass was turned up on its back in the grasp of that snake, so I ran down and rescued him, got that snake off of him. I stroked the bass to calm him down, fed him some worms, then put him back in the water and he swam away.

"The next day I was crossing the bridge and looked down to see that bass again, in a swirl of water near the bank, so I tossed him some more worms. This started happening almost every day till finally the bass started jumping out of the water when he saw me coming. I'd feed him worms and put him back in the creek, but one day I looked back as I was climbing the hill and saw that fish following me, walking as best he could on his fins. Shucks, I was afraid he'd die, so I carried him home and put him in a tub of water.

"He kind o' liked it there and it got so he'd spend as much time out of the tub as he did in it. He even got to eating with the dogs."

Truthful told how that fish got to tagging along with him all over the place, said it got real affectionate. But one day he was crossing that swinging bridge and looked back to see the fish fall through the bridge where a slat was missing.

"Boys," Truthful reported sadly, "that fish fell into Elkhorn Creek and drowned."

John Ed McConnell
ELKHORN, KENTUCKY

Big Catch

This fellow said he was fishing in a millpond and caught a catfish so large it took two mules to pull it out. He said the water dropped so rapidly in the pond, it caused the mill to turn backwards, and it unground ten bushels of corn.

Clarence Gillespie
BEREA, KENTUCKY

Jumpy

A fellow ran a mink farm. One day a tourist came by and asked, "How many skins can you get from each mink?"

"Just one," the fellow said. "They get kind of nervous if you try to skin them more than once."

Loyal Jones

Fairplay

Two fellows were playing cards, and suddenly one of them said, "Now play the cards fair, Reuben. I know what I dealt you."

The late Honorable Brooks Hays
LITTLE ROCK, ARKANSAS

Good Crop

A badman rushed into a barroom shooting his pistol into the ceiling and shouted, "All right, all of you bastards clear out of here."

Everybody ran out the door except for one fellow who stood nonchalantly drinking and who said, "Well, there shore was a bunch of them wudn't there."

Loyal Jones

Talking Dog

A fellow took a dog into a bar and announced that it could talk. The bartender asked what he could say.

The man said, "What's your name?" and the dog said, "Ruff, ruff."

"That's right, Ruff" the man said. "How are things?"

The dog said, "Ruff, ruff."

The man said, You're right. Things are rough. "Now, who is the greatest baseball player of all time?"

"Ruff, ruff," the dog said. The man said, "That's right, Babe Ruth," whereupon, the bartender threw them out.

When they got outside, the dog turned to the man and said,

"I knew I should have said Mickey Mantle."

Peter Hille
BEREA, KENTUCKY

Upsetting Experience

George met Bill on the road and said, "The sheriff shot my dog."

Bill said, "Was he mad?"

"Well, he wudn't too pleased about it, come to think of it."

Loyal Jones

RELIGION:

Sampson Slew the Philadelphians with the Assbone of a Mule?

I Believe you, Preacher

A fellow in the congregation was bad to exaggerate and out-right lie. The preacher decided to use a little psychology on him, and he told him a wild story about a feist terrier killing a grizzly bear. Then he asked the man if he believed the story.

"Oh yes," said the man, "that was my feist."

Rev. Ken Barker
ADDRESS UNKNOWN

Creatures Small

A little boy carrying a dead rat met a preacher, and he felt moved to tell the story of his hunting exploit. "Yeah, boy, I saw this old rat, and I grabbed up a big rock ..." Then recognizing the preacher, he finished with, "And then God called him home."

Muriel D. Miller
ADDRESS UNKNOWN

Matter of Elimination

This parishioner was dubious about the new pastor and asked a member of his previous church why he thought the man had gone into the ministry in the first place. His reply was,

"Well, he was too weak to plow, too dumb to teach, and too honest to law."

Loyal Jones

Which Zip Code

A joker called a convent and said to the the nun that answered, "This is Martin Luther."

Quick as a flash, she said, "Brother Martin, where in hell are you?"

Loyal Jones

Tit for Tat

A Sunday School teacher was teaching the Golden Rule. "It means we are here to help others," she said.

A little girl raised her hand and asked, "What are the others here for?"

Loyal Jones

Just Like Christ

Old Mr. Snodgrass got sick and went to the doctor, and after the good doc examined him, he said, "I'm so sorry to have to tell you this, but you are going to die in a very short time. If you need to get right with the Lord, you better do it because your time is very short."

"I've always been all right with the Lord, because I've always lived as near like Christ's life as I could," said Mr. Snodgrass.

"Can I do anything for you?" asked the doctor.

"Yes, you can call me a good lawyer."

The doctor called the highest priced lawyer in the city, and when he came in he stood on one side of the bed, and the doctor on the other.

"Do you want me to draw up a will for you?" the lawyer asked.

"No," answered the patient. "Since I've always lived like

Christ, I'd like to die just like he did, between two thieves."

Bonnie Collins
WEST UNION, WEST VIRGINIA

One of Ours

A Catholic and Jew worked side by side in a mill and got to be good friends. One day the Catholic came in smiling and said, "I'm so proud. My son is going into the priesthood."

"So what?" said the Jew.

"Well, he might become a bishop," said the Catholic.

"So what?"

"He might even become a cardinal."

"So what?"

"You know, he could become Pope."

"Will he ever be Jesus Christ?"

"Of course not."

"Well, one of our boys made it."

Bonnie Collins

Hampered

A Kentuckian living in Cincinnati had gone home to the mountains for the weekend. On Monday, someone asked if he had had a good time.

"Well," he said, "hit was all right except the preacher came home with us after church, and we had to eat the fried chicken with a knife and fork."

The late Dr. Raymond Drukker
BEREA, KENTUCKY

Ambiguous Verb

When I was pastor of the Stanford, Kentucky, Presbyterian Church, I usually answered the phone at the church by saying, "May I help you?"

One morning I was studying Corinthians 13 in preparation for Sunday's sermon. The phone rang. Without thinking, I picked it up and said, "May I love you?"

At first, no one responded. Then I heard someone clearing her throat, and it turned out to be one of the pillars of the church. She was eighty-three years old, and she forgot why she called. After I thought about it, I decided it was good theology.

Rev. Dan Clark
NICHOLASVILLE, KENTUCKY

Holiday Schmoliday

Three Japanese men, who had been in the United States for several years running auto plants, went golfing, and they played so hard that they all three had heart attacks and died. They arrived at the Pearly Gates to be met by St. Peter who was skeptical that they had been in the West long enough to learn much about Christianity. He decided to ask them a central question, "What is Easter?"

The first man said, "That's when you kill a turkey and have a big feast."

St. Peter said, "No, that's Thanksgiving."

The second man said, "That's when the fat guy brings presents."

"No, that's Christmas."

The third man said. "I know. That was when Christ was crucified between two thieves and died on Friday. They put Him in a tomb on Saturday. He rose and came out on Sunday, and if he saw his shadow, he had to go back for six more weeks."

Charlene Pullins
BEREA, KENTUCKY

Equitable

Three ministers, a Baptist, a Methodist, and an Episcopalian, were discussing how they divide up the collection. The Baptist said, "I take it down to the fellowship hall, draw a circle, throw the money up in the air. What falls within the circle goes to the Lord, and the rest I keep."

The Methodist said, "I take it down to the fellowship hall. There is a line down the center, and I throw it up in the air. What falls on one side of the line is the Lord's and the rest is mine."

The Episcopalian said, "We don't have a fellowship hall. We have a parish hall, but no circles or lines. What I do is throw it up in the air and say, 'Take what you want, Lord.' "

Rev. Carl Belden
VERSAILLES, KENTUCKY

The Stuff Marriage is Made Of

My father was a circuit-riding preacher in Boone County, West Virginia. He married a couple in the county seat of Madison one time, and then was gone on his rounds for two weeks. When he got back some fellows at the courthouse twitted him, "That couple you married has separated. You didn't tie the knot tight enough."

"I tied the knot tight, all right," my father replied, "but the material was a little weak."

Garland Stafford
STATESVILLE, NORTH CAROLINA

Whatever

Back in the last century before the temperance movement, some old-time Baptists would occasionally take a nip of the stronger stuff. A novice preacher was getting ready to do his first sermon, but he was very nervous. He asked an older preacher how he calmed his nerves. He told him that he took a small drink beforehand, and he took the young preacher out to his saddle-bags. He took a pretty stiff drink, and came back in and preached with a great deal of enthusiasm. Afterwards he asked the older preacher how he had done.

He said, "Well, you did pretty well, but I need to tell you that Sampson slew a thousand Philistines, not Philadelphians, and he slew them with the jawbone of an ass, not the assbone of a mule."

Loyal Jones

Tonsure

While the organ pealed bananas,
Lard was rendered by the choir.
After the sexton had rung the dishrag,
Someone set the church on fire.
"Holy Smoke," the preacher shouted
As his wig flew in the air.
Now his head resembles heaven
For there is no parting there.

Dr. John Ramsay
BEREA, KENTUCKY

Precautions

One day my dad and I were out plowing in the fields when my brother came running up from the house. He said, "Daddy, there's a preacher coming." Dad asked him which preacher it was, and he said he didn't know but he knew it was a preacher.

So Dad stood there a minute and said, "Son, I'll tell you what. I've got this plowing to finish, but it won't take long. Here's what I want you to do. Go back to the house, and if it's the Methodist preacher, I've got a twenty dollar bill lying on the dresser. You take that twenty dollars and put it in the sugar bowl and scoot it behind the flour.

"If it's the Presbyterian preacher, I've got a brand new gallon of homemade blackberry wine. I want you to take your toe and push that jug under the bed.

"Now, boy, if it's the Baptist preacher, I want you to climb up in your mother's lap and sit there until I get there."

Marc Pruett
ASHEVILLE, NORTH CAROLINA

Time to Repossess

Once upon a time a Baptist layman sold a cow to a comparative stranger with only a small downpayment. The buyer recommended himself for credit on the basis that he was a steward in the Methodist Church. The seller went home and asked his wife, "What is a Methodist steward?"

She replied, "Oh, he's about like a deacon in the Baptist Church."

Soon the Baptist layman was leaving the house, and his wife asked him where he was going.

He replied, "I'm going after my cow."

Rev. J. Harold Stephens
SHELBYVILLE, TENNESSEE

A Miracle

Three nuns were traveling through the mountains and ran out of gas. They remembered that they had seen a country store and gas station a mile or so down the road, so they hiked back to buy some gas. The store-owner had no container for them, so they shopped through the store, and the only container they could find was a chamber pot. So they bought it, filled it with gas and hiked back to their car. While they were pouring the gas into the vehicle, a farmer passed by, slowed, stopped, watched the operation, and said, "By golly, I'm a lifelong Baptist, but if that works I'm going to convert to your faith."

Victor Breedlove
MARBLE, NORTH CAROLINA

Too One-Sided

This true story happened in a Free Will Baptist Church, and a preacher told it to me. The congregation was having their Saturday business meeting, and the business at hand was the "churching" of one of the brethren. "Church" means to throw someone out of the church. This brother had been caught one time too many with another man's wife. Well, they were arguing back and forth about whether or not they ought to church the fellow. One side argued that they ought to get rid of this evil person and his evil influence. The other side argued that it was the responsibility of the church to forgive sinners and to bring them back into the fold. They weren't making a bit of progress toward solving the situation.

There was this old woman sitting in the back of the building, just taking it all in, and finally she had all she could take and she decided to have her say in the matter. She got the moderator's attention, and she stood up to say her piece, "I've been a member of this church for nigh onto forty years, and for forty years it's been 'Fornicate and forgive! Fornicate and forgive!' and I'm here to tell you good brethren and good sistern, I'm gittin' tired of being the one doing all the forgivin'!"

Peggy Davis
PIKEVILLE, KENTUCKY

Not Too Good

In the last century members of the Disciples of Christ and Churches of Christ were called Campbellites after one of their founders, Alexander Campbell. A young girl married an elderly Campbellite minister. A few months later one of her friends met her and asked how her marriage was.

"Not too good," she said. "The camel's died and the light has gone out."

Rev. William Hamilton, Sr.
BEREA, KENTUCKY

Delayed

Three women arrived at the Pearly Gates at about the same time. After checking in, they went for a tour of heaven. When they got back, they compared notes and agreed that heaven was the most wonderful place they had ever seen, with its golden streets, choirs, and beautiful music.

One of them said, "Just think, if we hadn't eaten all that oat bran, we could have been here three or four years ago."

Larry Sledge
BRANSON, MISSOURI

Any Change Would Be Nice

There was a man named Potter who lived over the Breaks of the Sandy in a remote area between Kentucky and Virginia, before the Interstate Park and the roads were built. He lived hard on a rocky farm. One day a preacher rode by and stopped to talk to him about religion. The preacher got to the main point and said, "The choice is yours. Will you spend eternity in heaven or Hell?"

Old Man Potter reflected and said, "Well, either one would be better than what I'm used to."

Hal Harlow
RICHMOND, KENTUCKY

Other Plans

In an old-fashioned tent meeting, the preacher went and put his arm around a stranger during the invitation hymn and said, "Don't you want to go to heaven with me?"

The fellow replied, "Well, I might, but I've made arrangements to move to Arkansas."

Rev. J. Harold Stephens
SHELBYVILLE, TENNESSEE

Washing Away Sins

This woman was baking light bread, and she took two loaves out of the oven and put them on the window sill to cool, it being summer. Two little boys came by, saw the loaves, and stole them. She took out after them, and they stuffed the loaves down in their shirts. That ran down to the river where a preacher was baptizing a couple of converts. They got in line, the preacher baptized one, and a loaf of bread floated up. He baptized the other one and the second loaf floated away.

A woman on the banks said, "You're doing good, Preacher, their sins are floating away in chunks!"

> *Rev. William Hamilton, Sr.*
> BEREA, KENTUCKY

Paying the Lord

A young preacher at Prestonsburg walked up to a much older townsman and said to him: "Mr. ____, the Lord is in need of money, and you owe him five dollars."

"Young fellow," replied the townsman, "I'm a lot older than you, and will see the Lord before you do, and will just hand him the five-spot myself."

> *The late Dr. Josiah H. Combs*
> PERRY COUNTY, KENTUCKY
> AND FT. WORTH, TEXAS

Life Ain't Always Living

Three preachers, a Baptist, a Methodist, and an Episcopalian, got into a discussion about when life begins. The Baptist thought it was at the moment of conception, and the Methodist thought it was at birth.

The Episcopalian opined, "It is when the kids leave home and the dog dies."

> *Dr. Robert Johnstone*
> BEREA, KENTUCKY

Another Hierarchy of Belief

A Methodist is a Baptist who can read and write. A Presbyterian is a Methodist who went to college. An Episcopalian is a Presbyterian who made it in society and whose deals all worked out. A Catholic is an Episcopalian who saw the light—and also managed not to flunk Latin.

> *The late Raymond Layne*
> BEREA, KENTUCKY

Revelation

The preacher was working mightily on his sermon. His daughter was watching, and she asked, "Daddy, does God tell you what to say?"

"Of course, child," he said. "Why do you ask?"

"Well then, why do you scratch some of it out?"

Raymond Layne

No Enemies

A young Methodist preacher held a two-week revival. The preacher preached well, the choir sang heavenly music, and many souls were converted. On the final Sunday evening, the preacher asked if any in the congregation had anything to say before the meeting closed. An old man in the front pew feebly rose with the help of his walker. He said he had heard a great deal of good concerning the pastor and had not been disappointed. Finally, before falling back to his seat, the old man said, "The only other thing I have to say is just that I am thankful to be ninety-two years old and not have an enemy in the world."

The pastor said, "I know we've been here two weeks and everybody is wore out, but I'm just so impressed by what this gentleman has said. Did you hear him? He is ninety-two and does not have an enemy in the world! Isn't that glorious? I really think he has a message to share with us, and I wonder if he would object if I call on him to just get up and tell us how a man can live such a life. How can he be ninety-two years of age and not have an enemy in the world?"

The pastor urged the old man back to his feet, "Please," he said, "take your time and tell us how it is possible for you to be ninety-two and not have a single enemy."

He tottered as he embraced his walker. Then he began, "Well, this will not take long, Preacher. I outlived the sonsabitches!"

Ron Gregory
CHARLESTON, WEST VIRGINIA

Blamed for Everything

The Sunday School teacher asked little Johnnie, "Where is God?" Johnnie didn't answer. She asked again, "Where is God?" He still did not answer. So she said to him, "Johnnie, I'm going to ask you one more time, where is God?"

Johnnie jumped up, grabbed his little brother by the hand, ran home and hid in the closet. His brother asked, "Why are we hiding in this closet?"

Johnnie said, "God is missing, and it looks like they're blaming us."

Nina Jones Cotton
SIERRA VISTA, ARIZONA

Stretching a Four-Letter Word

A small Methodist church in the Tennessee mountains was sent a preacher who had been educated at the Yale Divinity School. They were real proud. His first sermon was based on the letters in Y-A-L-E. He said that "Y" stood for youth, and he preached for twenty minutes on the promise of youth. "A" was for ardor for the Lord, another twenty minutes worth. "L" was for love, and another twenty minutes. He finished up with "E" for evangelism, and went on for twenty minutes more. The congregation was both exhausted and disgusted. The preacher, looking for a compliment, asked one lady on her way out, "Was my sermon effective?"

The lady stared at him and said, "I'm just glad that you didn't graduate from Tennessee Technological University."

Averill Kilbourne
BEREA, KENTUCKY

Great Religious Moment

A little boy was drawing in Sunday School. The teacher asked, "What are you drawing?"

"God," he said

The teacher said, "Nobody knows what God looks like."

"They will in a minute," the little boy said.

Jim Stafford
NASHVILLE, TENNESSEE

D(r)unkard

A drunk man got on a bus, dropped his change, and the bus driver had to pick it up. The man went back and said to a man wearing a clerical collar, "May I sit here, Father?"

The clergyman said, "I'm not a priest. I'm a Dunkard pastor."

The drunk said, "I believe that's what the bus driver called me."

Dr. Joe Evers
BEVERLY, KENTUCKY

Pious Pitch

An evangelist picked up a hitchhiker. He was driving a big Mercury, was behind time, and he took off with a squeal of tires. Then, not wanting to waste an opportunity, he turned to his passenger and asked, "Are you prepared to die?"

The hitchhiker jumped out of the car and ran off into the woods.

Anne Philips
PINNACLE, NORTH CAROLINA

No Predestinarian

A soldier from the hills was dubious about going into battle. The Calvinistic sergeant tried to reassure him, "If a bullet has your name on it, it will find you."

The soldier replied, "I know that, but its the ones with 'to whom it may concern' that worry me."

Loyal Jones

Beauty Ain't Easy

The preacher, seeing a little girl all dressed up on her way to Sunday School, said, "That is a beautiful dress. Look at all those nice bows and ribbons and those pleats and embroidered flowers."

The little girl said, "Thank you, but my mama says it's a bitch to iron."

Dr. Donald Hudson
BEREA, KENTUCKY

You Think That's Cussing?

A little boy running barefoot stubbed his toe, and he let off a few curse words.

The preacher was passing by and said, "Son, your language sends cold chills up my back."

The little boy said, "If you'd been here when Daddy hit his thumb with a clawhammer, you'd have froze to death."

Dudley Brooks
A VISITOR FROM MISSISSIPPI

Which Way?

The tombstone of Congressman Carl Goerch, in Raleigh, North Carolina, has this often-used verse as an epitaph:

As you are now
So once was I.
As I am now
Soon you shall be
Prepare for death and follow me.

Someone wrote on the tombstone with a marker:

To follow you I can't consent
Until I know which way you went.

Ann Wright
DANVILLE, VIRGINIA

Improving Quality

Two preachers were comparing their congregations. The first preacher glowed with pride at how many new members had joined over the past year.

The second preacher admitted that his congregation had not grown in size, but he added, "We had some pretty sorry Christians withdraw their membership last year."

Dr. John C. Wolff, Jr.
LEXINGTON, KENTUCKY

Outbidded

They had one old Brother here who was a long-winded fellow. If he could get three hours sleep, he could preach the other twenty-one. One of his "Amen Corner" friends would go to sleep, and that was expected, but this one snored and it was annoying. So the preacher gave this old man's grandson five cents to keep his grandfather awake. This worked all right for two Sundays, but the third Sunday the old man snored as usual.

The preacher stopped the child after church and said, "Son, why didn't you earn your five cents and keep your grandfather awake?"

And he said, "He gave me ten cents not to disturb him."

Honorable John E. Garner
WINCHESTER, KENTUCKY

Brother or Sister?

A preacher was riding through a rural area and came to a church with a large crowd assembled, apparently for a funeral. As he started to ride by, a man came up to him and said, "You're a preacher, are you not?"

He said he was, and the man said that their preacher had taken ill and they had no one to preach the funeral sermon. So the preacher said he'd be glad to do it. As he walked up the aisle, he noted that the coffin was closed. He turned to the man who had accosted him and whispered, "Is it a brother or a sister?"

The man whispered back, "Just a cousin."

Dick Poplin
SHELBYVILLE, TENNESSEE

Clockin' On

Fellow died and went to heaven and St. Peter was showing him around. They went down a huge hallway, and all over the hallway were clocks, and he said, "What's that all about, St. Peter?"

He said, "Well, there's a clock there for everyone who's alive on earth."

The man said, "But why are some running fast and some slow?"

St. Peter said, "Well, the more they sin the faster their clock goes, and the less they sin, the slower they go."

"Oh, yeah," he said. "I see Brother So-and-so's, in my church. It's going pretty fast, and Sister So-and-so's, it's not going very fast." He said, "Oh, by the way, where's Brother Billy Wilson's at?"

St. Peter said, "Oh that one. It's back in my office. I use it for a fan."

Billy Wilson
BOBTOWN, KENTUCKY

The Lord As A Farmer

A man moved into this southwest Virginia county and bought a farm that was so run down they almost gave it to him. The fields were rocky and full of broomsedge, rutted from erosion, the barns were rotten and caving in, the main house looked like it was bombed in Beirut.

But the man was a hard worker and blessed with patience and a green thumb. He built little retaining dams for irrigation, filled in the rutted creeks, fertilized the fields and cleared the rocks, repaired the main house and built new out buildings and fences. Within five years the farm looked like a showplace and its value has increased a thousand percent.

That's when the preacher came to visit.

He looked around in amazement and declared, "Well, sir, it is a pure wonder what you and the Lord have done with this place."

The farmer didn't like the preacher's holier-than-thou tone of voice, so he said dryly, "Yeah, and you should a' seen it when the Lord had it by hisself."

Chinquapin Jones
GRAVEL SWITCH, KENTUCKY

Fishing Baptists

When you go fishing, you'd better take two Baptist preachers. Because if you just take one, he'll drink all the beer. Take two and one won't drink in front of the other one!

Johnny Hylton
BEREA, KENTUCKY

Better Offer

A coal operator who had made a lot of money caught a plane out of Lexington for Asheville. When the plane got over the Smokies, there was a terrific thunderstorm and much turbulence. The coal operator was scared and prayed for deliverance,

"Oh Lord, if you'll deliver me safely, I'll give you half of what I own."

The plane landed safely, and as he was making his way through the airport, a Baptist preacher tapped him on the shoulder and said, "I heard your prayer and your promise on the plane. Since I am a preacher of the Gospel, I will be glad to collect half of your assets."

The quick thinking that had made the operator rich produced this reply:

"Oh, I made the Lord a better offer. I said if he ever saw me on an airplane again, I'd give Him everything I own.

Loyal Jones

The Lord is With Me

The preacher was on the old Asheville-Marshall highway going to a revival meeting on a dark rainy evening. He was running late, and on the right and left were high rock cliffs. Below the cliffs on the left was the French Broad River. The preacher came up behind a car, and there was no place to pass. The driver of the car was drunk and was weaving from one side of the road to the other. The preacher tried to pass, but each time the drunk would weave over onto the other side of the road. This went on for what seemed like hours. Finally, the preacher speeded up and swept around the drunk. His car skidded and went off the road, rolled completely over, and landed upright against a tree on the river's edge.

The drunk realized something was wrong. He stopped his car and staggered back to the place where the preacher's car had gone off the road. He peered over the bank and yelled, "Shay, is everything all right down thar?"

The preacher, realizing he was not dead, said, "Yes."

The drunk asked, "Are you alone?"

The preacher responded, "No, the Lord is with me."

The drunk said, "Well, tell him to come ride with me before you kill him."

Dr. Kenneth Israel
CANDLER, NORTH CAROLINA

DOCTORS AND HEALTH:

Migrating Headaches, Sick-As-Hell Anemia, and Other Medical Problems

Stupid Callers

A fellow came to work one day with both ears burned. A co-worker asked him what happened.

He said, "Well, I was pressing my pants with this hot iron, and somebody called me on the telephone. I got confused and put the iron to my ear."

"I see," said the co-worker, "but what happened to the other ear?"

"That happened when that darned fool called back."

> Dan Robinson
> CORBIN, KENTUCKY

Bad Accident

A fellow went into a bar for a drink with his right arm held in a very unnatural position, sort of straight out to the side curled down and touching his hip.

The bartender asked, "What happened?"

"I don't know what you mean," said the customer.

"I mean what kind of accident did you have?"

"I haven't had any kind of accident. What are you talking

about?"

"I mean why are you holding your arm like that?"

The fellow looked down at his arm and said, "Oh my gosh, I've lost my watermelon!"

Loyal Jones

Matter of Judgment

I made a house call over in the Smoky Mountains one time. It was not snowing when I left home, but when I got to the foot of the mountains, it was getting late and snowing pretty hard, and a friend of mine was there at his barn as I pulled up. I asked him if he would help me put on some chains, that I was going to make another house call at a certain man's house.

He asked, "Did he call you and ask you to make a house call?"

"Indeed he did," I responded.

My friend said, " I'll tell you one thing. If a doctor came out on a night like this, I sure would be afraid to take his medicine!"

Estill Muncy, M.D.
JEFFERSON CITY, TENNESSEE

Psychology

We are a real contrary people in Southern Appalachia. We like to argue. There was a young boy in Campbell County, coal mining country, and he was kind of puny, skinny, wasn't eating too good. A bunch of social workers fooled with him a little bit, got a dietician and all, but they couldn't get him to eat. So, they decided to bring him down to Knoxville to a psychologist.

They explained the problem to the psychologist, and he said, "No problem. I'll be glad to talk to this young man and see if we can get him to eat."

They sat down and talked a while, and the psychologist reported to the social workers, "I can see clearly the problem with this young man is that he has never had any dietary choices."

So he went back in, and the boy was sitting there all humped up. He said, "Johnny, what would you like to eat for supper?"

He said, "I ain't hungry."

The doctor said, "Fine, but if you could have anything on this earth to eat, what would you have for supper?"

The boy thought a minute, "I'd like a big plate of worms."

The doctor thought a minute, and turned to his nurse, said, "Go out and get us some worms."

She came back in with a dozen of the biggest old greasiest night crawlers you ever saw—about three-trout-per-worm worms. He slid the plate toward the boy and said, "Johnny, go ahead and enjoy your meal."

Johnny looked at him a minute, shoved them back over, and said, "I don't like to eat alone."

The doctor looked at him warily and said, "Well, I might join you a little bit."

Johnny said, "Well, I ain't hungry, but I might eat one."

The doctor picked up one, scraped the other eleven off of it and laid it in front of Johnny. Johnny said, "I told you I don't like to eat alone."

The doctor was getting nervous, but he took out his knife and cut the worm in two pieces. He picked up that grimy, slithering thing, dropped it into his mouth, and gulped it down.

Johnny burst into tears, and the doctor said, "Son what's wrong?"

Johnny screamed, "You ate *my* half!"

Sam Venable
KNOXVILLE, TENNESSEE

Frugal Last Words

An elderly man was being wheeled into the operating room for open heart surgery. He was told his chances for recovery were fifty-fifty. Suddenly he insisted that they page his wife so that he could issue his "last words" to her.

When she arrived he said, "Whatever happens to me, remember

don't pay over twenty dollars a cord for firewood."

Jonathan Greene
MONTEREY, KENTUCKY

Learning the Trade

Did you ever sit in a doctor's office and read the certificates and degrees that are always hanging there on the wall? One reads, "Dr. John is entitled to practice ..." You know reading that "to practice" just scares the hell out of a lot of people.

Lonnie "Pap" Wilson
NASHVILLE, TENNESSEE

Hold-Out

A doctor lived in a fine apartment house, and he came home in the dumps. His wife greeted him at the door, took his hand and said, "What's the matter, Dear? Bad day at the office?"

The doctor said, "No, it's that janitor on the first floor. He says he's made love to every woman in this building except one."

The doctor's wife said, "It must be that snooty Mrs. Freeman on the seventh floor."

Lonnie "Pap" Wilson

No-Show Cure

A Dr. Johnson was on trial for malpractice back in the days when doctors made house calls. His attorney had been busy rounding up former patients who could testify as to his healing prowess. Such a witness was put on the stand, and the defense attorney began examining him.

"I understand that Dr. Johnson saved your life?"

"Yes, he did," the witness said.

"Tell us how he saved your life," requested the attorney.

"Well, it was like this," he said. "I was real sick and sent for Dr. Jones. He gave me medicine, and I got worse. I sent for Dr. Phillips. He gave me more medicine and I got worse. In fact, I was near death, and then I sent for Dr. Johnson."

"And he came and cured you?"

"No, he never did come, and I think that's why I got well."

Loyal Jones

Ugly Bill Payer

The doctor examined the patient and then went out to talk to his wife. He said, "I don't like the looks of your husband."

She said, "I don't either, but he's good to the kids and is a good provider."

Loyal Jones

Extension

A doctor gave his patient six months to live, but he didn't pay his bill, and so he gave him six months more.

Loyal Jones

You've Got It

If you wheeze and sneeze and burn and freeze and barely breathe and feel weak in the knees,

If you hurt in the head and wish you were dead and your eyes are all red and your legs feel like lead,

If you can't eat a bite and you can't sleep at night and your chest is all tight and you look a sight,

If your throat is all raw and you ache in the jaw and there's no sand in your craw,

If you're feeling ill and you shake and you chill and you've lost all your will,

If your ears are roaring and your nose is pouring and you're heaving and snoring,

If you have an aching back and you cough and you hack and you're really on the rack,

If you stew and spew until your face turns blue, Man, you've got the flu!

Composed by Edward Ward
BLEDSOE, KENTUCKY

Slightly Messed Up

A psychotic thinks that two plus two is five.
A neurotic knows that two plus two is four, but he hates it.

A neurotic builds castles in the clouds.
A psychotic lives in them.
The psychiatrist collects the rent.

A neurotic is one who—
If single, wants to be married.
If married, wants to be single.
If at a wedding, wants to be the bride.
If at a funeral, wants to be the corpse.
If at dinner, dreams of sex.
And if in bed, wants ice cream.

Bob Hannah
ATLANTA, GEORGIA

Pill Peruser

A woman took her elderly father to a clinic for an examination, and when they went by the clinic pharmacy, she inquired, "Do you need any medicine, Daddy?"

"Well, I don't know," he said. "What have they got?"

Loyal Jones

Somebody's Got to Claim It

A man was taking tests in a hospital. A nurse asked him to take a bottle to the bathroom and bring her the result. He was shy, however, and he talked his wife into returning the bottle to the nurse.

"Is this urine?" the nurse asked.

"No, it's his'n."

Dan Greene
DAVID, KENTUCKY

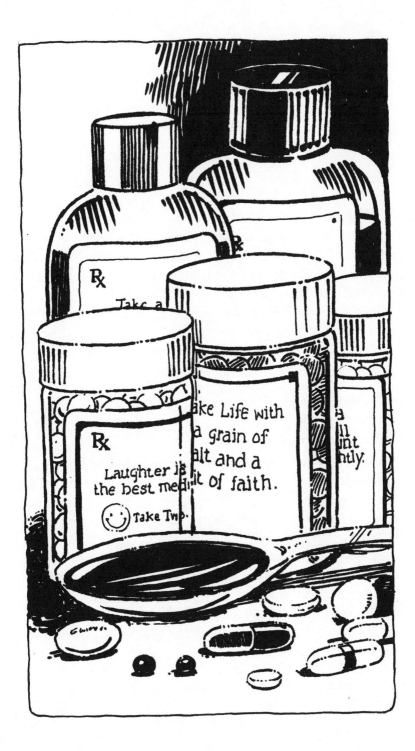

Medical History

A mountain woman came down to the university hospital for some tests. A doctor checked her over and then asked some questions. Are you sexually active?" he asked.

"Well," she said, "I try to be as still as I can."

Karen Sexton
LEXINGTON, KENTUCKY

Just What the Doctor Ordered

A fellow went to see his doctor with a crick in his neck. The doctor said, "Well, when I have a crick, I get in a hot shower with my wife and let the hot water run on it, and my wife massages it. That usually cures it. You might try that."

The fellow came back in a week or so, and the doctor asked, "Did you try that treatment I suggested?"

"Yes I did," the man said, "and it worked. Oh yes, by the way, you have a nice house."

Dr. Warren Lambert
BEREA, KENTUCKY

You'll be Ready to Go

This fellow down in the city was getting sicker and sicker. His doctor put him in the hospital and ran lots of tests. The doc walks in one day and says, "I've got good news and bad news. The good news is, we finally found out what's wrong with you. The bad news is that it's terminal."

"Terminal!" the man screamed. "How long have I got?"

"Best I can figure, about six months," the doctor answered.

"Then what should I do?"

The doc thought a minute. Finally he said, "If it was me, I'd give away everything I have here in the city. Then I'd move way back into the mountains and marry me a widow woman with fourteen children. I'd get up every morning before dawn and hitch up the old mule and plow those hills and try to scratch out a living."

"That'd help me live longer?" the patient wanted to know.

"Oh, Lord no!" said the doctor, "but that'll be the longest six months you ever spent!"

Sam Venable
KNOXVILLE, TENNESSEE

The Naked Truth: Doctor Knows Best

I went to see our psychiatrist up at Elkview, West Virginia this morning. We don't have a general practicing doctor—they seem to think they can't handle us—so we've got a psychiatrist instead, and his name is Dr. Sigmon Sizemore.

I said, "Dr. Sizemore, I've got a little throat trouble here and I've got to go down to Berea and be on a program tonight."

He said, "Go into that room and take off all of your clothes."

I said, "Doc, it's just in my throat!"

He said, "Now, are you gonna be the doctor, or am I gonna be the doctor?"

So I went ahead into the room and started taking off all my clothes, when I noticed a man sitting over in the corner on a stool, naked as a jaybird. I said, "Isn't this awful? I just came in for my throat and he's got me in here taking off all my clothes."

The guy said, "You're lucky, I just came in to tune the piano!"

George Daugherty
ELKVIEW, WEST VIRGINIA

Right Thing, Wrong Place

I have an elderly aunt who suddenly went stone deaf, just all at once.

So we took her to the doctor for an examination. It didn't take him long to find out what was wrong. "Mary," he said, "you've got a suppository in your ear."

She said, "Well I wonder what happened to my hearing aid?"

John Ed McConnell
ELKHORN, KENTUCKY

Armed and Dangerous

A lady drove her little boy from Gravel Switch into Harrodsburg one day, found the doctor's office and rushed in to declare, "Doctor, Doctor, my son Elmer here has swallowed a .22 shell. What are we gonna do?"

The doctor calmed her down, assured her Elmer would be all right, and told her, "Just take him back home and feed him a bottle of castor oil, and don't aim him at nobody!"

Chinquapin Jones
GRAVEL SWITCH, KENTUCKY

Heard at the Hospital:

- He quit breathing and they had to give him artificial insemination.
- A husband wanted to get his wife fitted with an I O U, but she was only interested in a monogram.
- A man said, "If anything happens, my son has the power of eternity."
- A lady said she felt lustless, and she also wanted something for ministerial cramps.
- One man complained of sick-as-hell-anemia, said he had endurable pain during intersection.
- A lady complained of migrating headaches and itches in the Virginia.
- One man requested a scat can of the brain, and another said he used Soybean Jr. for sore muscles.
- Then there was the guy who complained of pain in the palms of his feet.

Dr. Bryan E. Nelson,
a member of the Kentucky Club of
SOUTHERN INDIANA

He'd Cough A Mile for A Camel

There was a ninety-year-old man living in the North

Carolina mountains who had allegedly smoked two packs of Camels a day since he was 15 years old.

R. J. Reynolds, which makes Camels, heard of the man and sent a representative to see him. The Reynolds man asked if the old boy would come to Winston-Salem (Reynolds' headquarters) to make a commercial.

They would show anti-smokers that you could smoke and still live a long life. The old man agreed to make the commercial.

"Can you be in Winston-Salem at 9:00 Friday morning?" he was asked.

"Nope," said the old man.

"Why not?" asked the Reynolds man.

"'Cause I don't quit coughing until 12."

The Late Lewis Grizzard
ATLANTA, GEORGIA

Keep the Change

Wayne Carson, who wrote "You Were Always On My Mind," called Producer Ray Baker early one a.m. and said he was in trouble. Ray asked him what was wrong.

Wayne said, "I just woke up in a confused state. I had my pills and some change on the night stand." Said, "I just took 40 cents!"

Billy Edd Wheeler

Flunked Anatomy

This physician I work for plays a game with his young patients to test their knowledge of body parts. One day he pointed to a little boy's ear and asked, "Is this your nose?"

The child turned to his mother and said, "I think we better find a new doctor."

Adam Broadus
NEW ALBANY, INDIANA

In the Apple Orchard

On the very head waters of South Hominy Creek, the deer were so numerous that some had to be eliminated. A Mr. Warren, therefore, started killing deer with his rifle. One day he wounded a deer, and it became very mad. He charged Mr. Warren and gouged him in the groin area. His sister, Cindy Warren, ran a mile to the nearest telephone and called Dr. Rich's office. Huffing and puffing, she explained that her brother was bad hurt. She kept on talking and explaining that Dr. Rich must hurry. Dr. Rich finally asked her, "Where was Mr. Warren hurt?"

Her immediate response was, "In his apple orchard."

> *Harry O'Kelly*
> *(provided by Kenneth Israel)*
> CANDLER, NORTH CAROLINA

Psycho-Whatever

I am a psycho-neuro-immunologist. I finally found out what I am. Dr. Sigmund Sizemore, our psychiatrist and general practice doctor up at Elkview, West Virginia, he told me that's what I am. That's what all us humorists are. Norman Cousins' book proves that, and the other guys writing about humor and health agree with what Dr. Sizemore has been saying all these years:

> If you live, laugh, love and be happy, consider the lilies of the field, and if you consider just today and not worry about tomorrow, your brain is making you well from diseases you don't even know you've got. It's sending stuff out to your organs that makes you feel good and which doesn't give you a hangover like drugs and alcohol.

Dr. Sizemore writes little messages like that for the Elkview News and World Report. The other day he wrote this on the front page,

> He was a cautious man; he never romped and played.
> He never smoked, he never drank, he never kissed a maid.
> And when he up and passed away, his insurance was denied.

They said, "That guy never lived, so we claim he never died."

Dr. Sizemore doesn't miss much. He also said, "Everybody's worth something, even if it's only as a bad example."

George Daugherty
ELKVIEW, WEST VIRGINIA

No Miracles for Me

Three fellows were walking along when an angel suddenly appeared before them and said, "I can grant you each a wish."

The first one said, "I've got terrible arthritis. It gives me pain all the time, and I can't get around like I used to. Can you cure it?"

The angel said, "You're cured," and the man went off flexing his arms and legs.

The second one said, "I've got heart trouble and I can't do anything strenuous. I'd like for you to cure it."

The angel said, "You're cured," and he skipped off happily.

The angel looked at the third fellow, who threw up his arms, backed of, and said, "Get away from me. I'm on full disability."

Tom Bonny
IRVINE, KENTUCKY

OLD AGE:

The Gleam in Your Eye
is the Sun Hitting Your Bifocals

Nearly All There

I like my bifocals,
My dentures fit me fine.
My hearing aid is perfect,
But, Lord, how I miss my mind!

Nina Jones Cotton
SIERRA VISTA, ARIZONA

Hereafter

The preacher came to call the other day. He said at my age I
ought to be thinking about the hereafter. I told him, "Oh, I do all
the time. No matter where I am—in the parlor, upstairs, in the
kitchen, or down in the basement, I ask myself, 'Now, what am I
here after?' "

Lewis Lamb
PAINT LICK, KENTUCKY

Silence is in the Nose of the Beholder

This is fresh from Roane County fiddler Frank George. It
seems this older neighbor of Frank's went to the doctor complaining of "silent gas." She'd been passing silent gas a lot lately,

including several times since she had been in the doctor's office.

"First thing," the doctor told her, "we're going to get you a hearing aid."

Ken Sullivan
CHARLESTON, WEST VIRGINIA

Half and Half

An elderly fellow went to the doctor for an examination. The doctor said, "You're going to have to give up about half of your love life."

"Which half?" the man asked, "thinking about it or talking about it?"

Loyal Jones

Slow Learner

My great-grandfather James Farmer was a surveyor of large tracts of land in Bell, Harlan and Letcher Counties and was a representative in the state legislature as well as county surveyor. He was also something of a sage and wit.

He had one failing. He liked to drink whiskey and would get on some real stemwinders. Getting over one of these bouts with the bottle, he would just about die for a few days and would have to lie in bed and mope about the house.

The funny thing was that just as soon as he got over a bad hangover, he would get hold of a jug of whiskey and get drunk again, with the same results.

One day a neighbor's wife, who was the mother of eleven children, said to him, "Mr. Farmer, when you get drunk and it just about kills you, what makes you turn around and get on another drunk?"

He answered, "When you have a baby and it just about kills you, then what makes you turn right around and have another one?"

Col. Edward Ward
BLEDSOE, KENTUCKY

Who Was That ...?

An elderly man took daily walks in the park of a small town, and one day he saw a really good looking older woman and thought he'd like to get to know her. The next day it so happened that she was walking in front of him. He caught up with her and began to chat, found out a little about her and finally invited her to dinner. They ate at a nice place, had a lot in common, and so he invited her to go dancing. Before the evening was over, he proposed to her, took her home, thanked her for a nice evening and went home. Then he couldn't remember what her answer was when he proposed. He couldn't sleep for worrying, and the first thing next morning, he called and asked,

"What was your answer when I asked you to marry me?"

"Oh, I accepted," she said, "but I'm glad you called, because I had forgotten who asked me."

Dr. Stanley Wall
LEXINGTON, KENTUCKY

Who Needs It?

An old man, maybe eighty-five years old, was playing a round of golf. He had to play by a swampy place with water, and when he walked by he saw a frog sitting in the water. The frog said, "I am an enchanted princess. Kiss me and I will turn into my beautiful former self, and you may do what you will with me."

The old man picked up the frog and put it into his pocket and played another hole of golf.

The frog said from his pocket, "Hey, kiss me and I will turn into a beautiful princess, and I'll do anything you want me to do."

The old man ignored the frog and played another hole. The frog got pretty upset and said,

"Hey, old man, I said kiss me and I'll do anything for your pleasure."

The old man said, "At my age I'd rather have a talking frog."

Glenda White
BEREA, KENTUCKY

Time Share

An older man proposed to marry a much younger woman, so there was considerable discussion about the arrangements:

YOUNG WOMAN: I want my own checking account!
OLD MAN: OK!
YOUNG WOMAN: I want to TRAVEL a lot!
OLD MAN: Fine! I like to travel too!
YOUNG WOMAN: I want to be IN CHARGE of this marriage!
OLD MAN: That's all right by me. You are in charge!
YOUNG WOMAN: I want SEX EVERY NIGHT!
OLD MAN: OK! Put me down for Wednesdays!

James Gay
LAKEWOOD, PENNSYLVANIA

No Rush Orders

Two old people met in a nursing home. One of them asked, "What is your name?"

The other one said, "How soon do you need to know?"

Loyal Jones

How Old?

This fellow claimed he was so old that they didn't teach history when he went to school. There wasn't any.

Rollie Carpenter
WINCHESTER, KENTUCKY

Slap-Start

Two women in a retirement home were talking about a date one of them had had with a fellow resident the night before.

"I had to slap him three times," she said.

"You mean, he got fresh with you?" the other asked.

"No, I thought he was dead!"

Loyal Jones

A Problem, Doc

A man went to see his doctor and said, "My wife's got a problem. I talk to her, and she doesn't answer. She's getting hard of hearing."

The doctor said he needed some idea about how hard of hearing she was and suggested that he go back home and sort of test her hearing at different distances and report back to him.

So the man went home, opened the front door and called, "Hi, Honey, what are we having for supper?" No answer.

He took four or five steps into the house and called again. "Hi, Honey, what are we having for dinner?" No answer.

He went on into the dining room and said the same thing again. No answer. He went on into the kitchen, said the same thing, and his wife yelled, "You deaf old goat, I told you three times, meatloaf!"

Governor Brereton Jones
FRANKFORT, KENTUCKY

No Need to Write it Down

Aunt Mavis and Uncle Arlo—they're getting up in years now—but they were sitting out on the porch the other evening, just rocking. She said, "You know what I would like to have?"

He said, "What?"

She said, "A big bowl of vanilla ice cream with chocolate sauce on it."

He said, "Boy, that would be good!"

She said, "A big bowl of vanilla ice cream with chocolate sauce on it, and maybe some nuts."

He got up and started off, "I'll go down to the drugstore and get us some."

She said, "Now that's vanilla ice cream, with chocolate sauce, with nuts on it. Better write it down."

He said, "I don't need to write it down. I can remember that."

About forty-five minutes later he was back with two ham sandwiches. She said, as he handed her one and she looked at it. "You dummy, I told you to write it down. I wanted mustard on mine!"

Dr. Carl Hurley
LEXINGTON, KENTUCKY

Strangers

A tour bus broke down on the road, and the travelers went to a nearby motel to arrange rooms. There were enough rooms for everybody except this one woman. She asked the motel manager if he couldn't do something.

He said, "Well, there is one single man in the party, and he has a couch in his room. You might ask him if you could sleep there."

So she went to the man's room and knocked and asked if she might sleep on his couch.

He said, "Look, I don't know you. You don't know me. We don't know any of these other people. And they don't know us. I don't see why not."

She moved in, and they chatted for a few minutes, he went to the bathroom, came out in his pajamas and went to bed. She went to the bathroom, changed into her nightgown and lay down on the couch. Tossed around on the couch, couldn't sleep.

Finally she said, "This couch is lumpy and hard and I can't get comfortable. Do you think it would be all right if I just lay on top of the covers on the other side of your bed?"

He said, "Look, I don't know you. You don't know me. We don't know any of these other people, and they don't know us. I don't see why not."

So she got up on top of the covers beside him. She lay there for some time and then said, "I'm cold. I can't sleep. Do you think it would be all right if I got under the covers? I'll stay on my side of the bed."

He said, "Look, I don't know you. You don't know me. We don't know any of these other people, and they don't know us. I don't see why not."

So she got under the covers, lay there a while and said, "Would you like to have a party?"

He said, "Look, I don't know you. You don't know me. We don't know any of these other people, and they don't know us. Who would we invite?"

Hilda Woodie
BEREA, KENTUCKY

Would've Been More Careful

One old fellow said that if he'd known he was going to live until he was ninety, he'd have taken better care of himself. Another one asked him how he had spent his money. He said, "Some I spent on liquor, some on women, and the rest I spent foolishly."

Loyal Jones

You Know You're Getting Older When ...

The following have been contributed by various people in various forms and have been widely reprinted.

- You don't care where your wife goes as long as you don't have to go with her.
- The little old lady you help across the street is your wife
- Everything hurts, and what doesn't, won't work
- The gleam in your eye is the sun hitting your bifocals
- Your knees buckle but your belt won't
- You get winded just playing checkers
- You feel like the night before, but you haven't been anywhere
- You look forward to a dull evening
- You sit down in your rocking chair, and you can't get it started

- Your little black book contains only names ending in M.D.
- Your back goes out more than you do
- You decide to procrastinate but never get around to it
- You know all the answers but nobody asks you the questions
- Your children begin to look middle-aged
- You walk with your head held high trying to get used to your trifocals
- Your mind makes contracts your body can't keep
- You finally get it all together but can't remember where you put it
- You have more hair on your chest than on your head
- You turn out the lights for economic rather than romantic reasons
- The best part of your day is over when the alarm clock goes off
- It takes an hour to dress and another to remember why
- After painting the town red, you have to recuperate before giving it a second coat
- Your midnight oil is all used up by nine o'clock
- You get your exercise being a pallbearer for friends who exercised
- Any change you drop less than a quarter isn't worth bending over for
- Dialing long distance wears you out
- Your main squeeze is the Charmin
- You just can't stand people who are intolerant
- You sink your teeth into a steak and they stay there
- Your pacemaker makes the garage door go up when a pretty girl goes by
- You finally get to the top of the ladder, but it's leaning against the wrong wall
- You've got too much room in your house and not enough in your medicine cabinet.

SAYINGS, DIALECT, AND RIDDLES:

His Cheese Done Slid off his Cracker

Dialect

Sam Venable, humor columnist for the *Knoxville News-Sentinel* has a great talk about Appalachian pronunciation and use of words. Here are some of his and we've added a few more.

Tawlk	That's what we do when we say words. I never did know we tawlked funny until I went outside the region, and heard how funny everybody else tawlks.
Tar	What goes on your car. Most cars have four of them—unless they're up on sinner blocks—one white wall, two black walls and one racing slick.
Sinner	I just told you, sinner blocks, but it's got another meaning like the middle of something. I'm in the sinner of the stage ritcheer.
Flares	Like what you give a girl or put on graves.
Share	A kind of bath. "I took two shares today because it was ninety in the shade."
Shore	Of course. Note that shore and share mean two different things.
Mere	What you look in when you get out of the share.
Barred	We had two bankers that barred money from

155

folks and never did pay it back. That's because they didn't know the basics of mine: urine, hisn and hern (see below). They gave them a few years to learn it.

Shurf — Who you call if you have a flat tar in the country.

Please — Who you call if you have a flat tar in the city.

Testes — That's what you take to get a grade. You sit at deskes to take testes.

Noed — To be aware of. "I noed she was going to give us testes today!"

Adder — Not a snake. It means a later time. "I'll get a job adder hunting season is over."

Brang — Fetched. As in bring, brang, brung.

Flash — Not like lightning but like flash and blood. "There he was in the flash."

Far — The hot stuff like you have in Hale.

Hale — A place you're sent to if you're bad, where all the far is.

Hale Far — An expletive. "Well, hale far, I never noed I's going that fast."

Fartar — What you get up in to look for fars.

Bobwar — That what they put around fartars to keep people from stealing copper pipe out of the toilets for 4-H projects, or something, out in the woods.

Wranch — Several meanings. You can wranch your knee jumping bob war fences. It's also a tool you work on a '47 Ford with.

Ranch — What you do to clothes after you warsh them. You ranch them out a little bit.

Clim — This is the past tense of climb. "I clim that ridge 'til my tongue lolled out." Sometimes clum.

Nem — As when you're driving down the road, you see your neighbor, and you roll down the window

	and yell, "How's your Mom an'em doin'?"
Yale	How you get somebody's attention. You yale at them.
Bale	Something that rangs.
Cheers	That's what you set on.
Lag	A cheer has four lags.
Bubs	What you plant to get flares. Another kind of bubs is them that light up, iffen you got 'lectric pare.
Pare	What the TVA brung.
Shed	Like divorce. "She done got shed of him."
L-I-B	What people say when they hear she done got shed of him: "L-I-B, I didn't know that!"
Air	A unit of time. "He's done been gone a air." Sometimes means thar. Like, "Go shet that-air door."
Ort	As in, "You ort to go see your Mama."
Wangs	Them's what birds use to fly.

Medical and Health Dialect

Very Close Veins	They swell up too.
Risin'	Not like getting up in the morning. Like a boil. Heard a doctor call it "an inflammation of the subcutaneous tissue." What's that supposed to mean?
Breaking out	Not out of jail. Related to risin'. Pimples all over ye.
Genital Heart Disease	The worst kind.
Insensitive Care Unit	Where they keep you when you real sick.
Leaders	Not them guys in the White House. Tendons.
Make Water	Not like a chemist. Pee.
Old Arthur	That Greek ailment, arthritis.

Right Smart	Not about being smart. Means you got a lot of whatever you got.
Stove Up	Not putting a stove together. Means you stiff and sore from whatever you did too much of.
Trots	Not a horse race. Means you ain't moseying to the outhouse. Dierear.
Running Off	Same thing.
Back Door Quickstep	Same thing again.
Barium	What you do when you can't cure 'em.
Congenital	Real friendly.
Dilate	Opposite of when you die early.
Outpatient	One that fainted.
Secretion	You hiding something.
Urine	Not mine, his'n or her'n. Your'n.
Nerves	All shook up and jumpy.
In a Swivet	Same thing.
In a Tizzy	Same thing.
Tore Up	Same thing.
All to Pieces	Same thing again.
All Overs	Same thing but with goose bumps.
Down in the Dumps	Not picking through the trash. The mully-grubbing blues.
Old Timer's Disease	CRS (Can't remember stuff).
Enemies	Them disgusting flush-jobs you get in the horspital. Come to think of it, also them that do it. *(Byron Crawford)*
Sinus	Pronounced seen-us. Real health problem. Like, "I was taking a joy-ride with my neighbor's wife, and he seen us."

Sayings

• Nineteen sheriffs in east Tennessee have gone to Federal prison for running dope. That's why they call them the "High

Sheriffs" *(Sam Venable)*.
- Nobody is too poor to own a dog. Some are so poor they have ten or fifteen.
- If all the economists were laid end to end, it would probably be a good thing *(Jim Reed)*.
- He was so lazy he wouldn't holler "sooey" if the hogs were eating him.
- He's so slow and lazy dead flies won't fall off him.
- He was so ugly his mother borrowed a baby to take to church.
- He fell out of the ugly tree and hit every limb on the way down.
- She was born ugly, but then she backslid.
- It's true that he is ugly, but he's stupid too.
- He was so ugly he had to whip his feet to get them into the bed with him at night.
- She was so ugly if you threw her in the lake you could skim ugly for a month *(Bill Foster)*.
- He was so ugly he had to sneak up on a glass of water to get a drink.
- She's over-egged her pudding *(Hon. Brooks Hays)*.
- All marriages are happy. It's the living together afterwards that's the problem.
- Don't never go around with another man's wife unless you can go three rounds with her husband *(Lonnie "Pap" Wilson)*.
- If thine enemy offend thee, buy his children a drum, a fiddle and an accordion.
- Marriages are made in heaven, but so are thunder and lightning *(Dottie Coe)*.
- Bigamy — Having one wife too many.
- Monogamy — Same thing.
- Anybody that marries for money earns every d___ penny of it.
- When they operated on my pappy, they opened my mammy's male *(Lonnie "Pap" Wilson)*.
- Conference - A means of substituting talk for work.

- She didn't want to marry him for his money, but there was no other way to get it *(Raymond Layne)*
- The only thing he ever did behind his wife's back was to zip her up *(Jim Reed).*
- People are down on what they are not up on *(Dan Allen).*
- It could have gone either way, and it did *(Gary Muledeer).*
- She's a few pickles short of a jar.
- He's two bricks shy of a load.
- He's a bubble off of plumb.
- He ain't got all his marbles.
- All her marbles ain't rolling in the same groove.
- He's got a screw loose.
- His cheese done slid off his cracker.
- His traces ain't hooked up right.
- She was as flaky as a bowl of Wheaties.
- He didn't have a full bucket.
- He's long on drywall and short on studs.
- The light's on but nobody's home.
- Her trolley has jumped the track.
- His elevator don't go all the way to the top.
- She's not wrapped too tight.
- His telephone's ringing but nobody's home.
- I don't believe her yeast rose.
- He's living in a hundred watt world with a forty watt bulb.
- I believe he's got a short in his cord.
- She's not wearing a full string of beads.
- He's playing baseball with a warped bat.
- He's a lost ball in the high weeds.
- She's two dishes short of a picnic.
    (Thanks to Carol Elizabeth Jones for some of the above)
- If you think it's a problem now, just wait till the government has solved it.
- Tomorrow is the longest day in the week, because of the things we're going to do then.
- Up North you have two seasons, winter and road construction.

- Why is it that "fat chance" and "slim chance" me thing? (*Eugene L. Smith*)
- All nuts ain't hanging from trees.
- I may appear to be bald, but that's a solar panel fc machine.
- Drinking whiskey removes blemishes and wrinkles—not from you but from the people you're looking at (*Judge Ray Corns*).
- Her stack cake was so good that if you slapped some on your forehead, your tongue would beat your brains out trying to get to it.
- He's economical with the truth; that's why he uses it so sparingly.
- I feel a whole lot more like I do now than I did a while ago (*Gene Burton*).
- Skeletons ain't nothing but a stack of bones with the people scraped off (*Virginia Kilgore*).
- He's so tall he has to climb a ladder to shave himself.
- And his feet are so big he has to put his britches on over his head.
- In fact, they were so big he had to go out in the field to turn around.
- She is prettier than a speckled pup with red eyeballs.
- Sorriest president we ever had—a pimple on the tail-end of progress.
- As long as I've got a biscuit, you got half.

You May Be From Appalachia If ...

The following items were mailed to me by someone who is unremembered. Some were dropped because of their negative qualities, but some are worth sharing, and I have added a few. (L.J.)

- You ever sprayed your girlfriend's name on an overpass.

ou consider a six-pack and a fly swatter quality entertainment.
- Someone asks for your I.D. and you show them your belt buckle.
- The primary color of your car is Bondo.
- Directions to your house include "turn off the paved road ..."
- Your dog and your wallet are both on a chain.
- You ever traded dogs and got boot.
- You owe the taxidermist more than your annual income.
- You have lost a tooth opening a beer or pop bottle.
- Your wife's hair-do has ever been ruined in a ceiling fan.
- You have a rag, an Irish potato or a cob for a gas cap.
- You have a groundhog or cat skin banjo head.
- You have ever barbecued Spam on your grill.
- Redman Tobacco sends you Christmas cards.
- You prominently display a gift you bought at Graceland.
- Your front porch has collapsed and killed more than three dogs.
- Anyone from your family has ever worn a tube top to a wedding.
- You have a picture of Conway Twitty, Loretta Lynn, or
  George Jones over the fireplace.
- You still have an eight-track tape in your truck.
- You've ever been to a funeral where there are more pick-up
  trucks than cars.
- You have any relatives named Homer, Fred, Clara Belle, Ethel,
  Gladys, Buford, or Woodrow.
- You have a cousin who moved up north and named her kids
  Brittany, Ashley, Jason, or Shawn.

Riddles

Riddles were a great part of early home and school entertainment, usually rhymed and requiring imagination and logical-illogical thought. Even in an age of multi-media entertainment, they persist. Some retain an Old World flavor. Most of the following riddles were collected by children in the White Hall Elementary School, Madison County, Kentucky.

A hill full, a hole full,
Yet you cannot catch a bowl full?
(Mist) *Mary Johnson*

What's black and white
And red all over?
(A newspaper) *Cie Shepherd*

What's round as a biscuit
And deep as a cup
The Cumberland River can't fill it up?
(A sifter or sieve) *Tyler Sanslow*

Black within and red without,
Four corners round about?
(Chimney) *Mary Johnson*

Formed long ago, yet made today,
Employed while others sleep.
What few would like to give away,
Nor any wish to keep?
(A bed) *Mary Johnson*

Purple, yellow, red and green,
The king cannot reach it, nor can the queen,
Nor can Noll, whose power is so great.
Tell me this riddle while I count eight.
(Rainbow) *Mary Johnson*

A water there is I must pass,
A broader water never was,
And yet of all waters I ever did see
I pass over it with less jeopardy.
(Dew) *Mary Johnson*

Black as a hole,
Slick as a mole,

Big long tail
And a thump hole?
(Iron skillet) *Tyler Short*

Round as a ring,
Deep as a spring,
Has taken the life
Of many a pretty thing.
(Rifle)

What walks on four legs at morning
Two at noon, and three at evening?
(A person, crawling as a baby, upright as adult, and old
with a cane)

White as milk and milk it ain't,
Green as grass and grass it ain't,
Red as blood and blood it ain't,
Black as ink and ink it ain't
(Blackberry)

How far can a dog run into the woods?
(Halfway. After that he's running out)
Billy Wilson

If you are in a room surrounded by mirrors, with a table in the
middle and no doors or windows, how would you get out?
(You look in the mirror, you see what you saw, you cut the
table in half with the saw, you put it back together again to
make it whole, you climb through the whole and you are out.)

Brandon Lilly

Quotations

It was so hot in Knoxville one time ... you know how hot it was?
It was so hot that two trees were fighting over the same dog!

Bill Anderage
KNOXVILLE, TENNESSEE

Laughter is like the human body wagging its tail.

Chinquapin Jones
GRAVEL SWITCH, KENTUCKY

She's awful pretty, but pretty don't make the pot boil.

Mary Isabelle Stewart
BEREA, KENTUCKY

The back pays for what the mouth eats.

John Payne
DISPUTANTA, KENTUCKY

Don't take no more on your head than you can kick off at your heels.

Aunt Ginny Wilson
PEACH CREEK, WEST VIRGINIA

Spare me from being one of the sad average.

Emily Ann Smith
BEREA, KENTUCKY

My crops didn't turn out as well as I thought they would. But then, I didn't think they would.

Chinquapin Jones
GRAVEL SWITCH, KENTUCKY

Boys, I just can't get ahead. I bring it in the front door with a thimble ... she throws it it out the back with a shovel.

Chinquapin Jones

Sermons, Speeches, and other Backwoods Oratory

Before movies, radio, and television, people had to provide their own entertainment, or seek it wherever it could be found. Sermons and speeches might enlighten and inspire listeners, but they also could highly entertain them. People would travel large distances to revivals, camp meetings, political gatherings, or Chautauqua-like events that might lift them out of the ordinariness of life.

Some preachers and speakers, knowing that people craved entertainment, ventured into excessively colorful language and delivery. They knew that it was a good idea to be humorous as well as eloquent if they were to hold their audiences. There were those also who loved to imitate preachers and orators and other public figures. Thus, among a people stereotyped as taciturn (or as one clinician put it, "non-verbal"), you find people who delight in language and all that you can do with it. Since Appalachians are storytellers, we actually have always valued language, and while we are known for the understated story, some can gild the lily when it comes to speech. Here are some examples.

THE PEEZLETREE SERMON

There are a good many sermon parodies in the oral tradition in Appalachia and the South. Several, including "The Peezletree Sermon," as well as "The Harp of a Thousand Strings," and "Where the Lion Roareth and the Whang-Doodle Mourneth for its First-Born" were credited to William P. Brannan, an itinerant typesetter and writer in the early nineteenth century. A version of "The Peezletree" was recorded by Holman Willis on Dialect Records (CB 057396). This kind of humor is based on the assumed ignorance of unschooled preachers who ventured beyond their knowledge of the scriptures. Of course, there are other stories that make fun of the stiff and proper seminary-trained preachers.

Bretheren and Sisteren, I been so busy this week with pastoral duties amongst the flock and a-gleanin' in the Vineyard of the Lord, that I ain't had no time to prepare no theologic sermon. So, I'm a-goin' to let this Old Bible drap open here, and wherever my eye lights, I'll take that as a sign that the Lord wants me to preach on that text and that He will revelate my mind so's that I can hold forth this mornin'.

My eyes light here, Bretheren and Sisteren, on a text as recorded in Two-I Kings whar it says, "The Chil'ern of Israel worshiped the Lord wi' the heart, wi' the instrument of the seb'n strings, and with the (here he hesitates and spells out the word) p-s-a-l-t-r-y" (and starts over). It says here, "The children of Israel worshiped the Lord wi' the heart, wi' the instrument of the seb'n strings and wi' the p-s-a-l-t-r-y ... oh, and wi' the peezletree." Now my text this beautiful Sabbath morning will be "The Peezletree."

I've done a great deal of studyin' about the history of the peezletree. The peezletree was a tree that growed up in Moses' backyard down in the land of Egypt, and when that peezletree growed up and flourished, Moses went out in his backyard and took out his two-bit Barlow knife, the one wi' four blades and a co-cola opener on the back, and he cut hisself a walkin' stick off'n the peezletree. And when he'd trimmed his stick up good and smooth-ah, the Lord spoke unto him and said, "Moses, take thy peezletree staff in thy right hand, and put thy foot slap-dab in the middle of that big road that leads on down to Mr. Pharaoh's house-ah!" Now, Bretheren and Sisteren-ah, Pharaoh was quality folks in them parts in them days down in Egypt, but Moses he ain't payin' no mind to that, 'cause he knowed that the Lord was behind him, and he walked big and bold-ah, Bretheren and Sisteren, like the Lord wants his people to walk when they goin' about His business!

Moses, he jus' walked right up to the front door of Mr. Pharaoh's house, and knocked wi' that big brass knocker, and when the hired-girl come to the door-ah, she said, "What do you mean, Moses, a-comin' up here knockin' on quality-folks' front door like this?" Pharaoh was a proud man. He don't like to have people a-knockin' on his front door. But Moses just said, "I want to see Old Pharaoh," but that girl said, "Mr. Pharaoh claims he ain't in this mo'ning." Moses he said, "I know he's in, 'cause I seen his saddlehorse hitched up to the fence out there-ah."

Bretheren and Sisteren, Moses he just walked right in through the livin' room, down the hall and into the kitchen where Pharaoh was a-sittin' at the kitchen table drinkin' his coffee.

Old Pharaoh said, "Moses, what you doin' pesterin' me so early in the mornin' when quality folks ain't had their second cup of coffee yet?"

Moses said, "Pharaoh, I want you to turn them chil'ren loose-ah."

Pharaoh said, "What chil'ren you talkin' about?"

Moses said, "Now, Pharaoh, don't you try to act like no big-shot wi' me. You know I'm a-talkin' about them Chil'ren of Israel, that I want you to turn a-loose-ah!"

Pharaoh said, "What ye mean a-talkin' about them Chil'ren of Israel for? Didn't I give them a day off on Washington's Birthday, and didn't I give them the Fourth of July off, and ain't the corn and t'baccer just filthy wi' weeds?"

When Moses seen that Old Pharaoh was a-hardenin' his heart 'ginst him like that, he just throwed his peezletree walkin'-stick down there on the floor-ah, and it turned into a great big old fiery serpent! Pharaoh jumped back. He's scared! And Moses, he just reched out and took up that fiery serpent by the tail and twisted it around Pharaoh's head three times, and then he took the charm off, and that snake turned back into a peezletree walking stick.

Then Pharaoh said, "Now looky here, Moses, whilst you was a-talkin', I was a-studyin' on this thing-ah. Let's talk sense now. Them Chil'ren of Israel is purty triflin' field hands anyhow, and they done et more than they's worth. I'm a-goin' to let them Chil'ern go!"

And Moses, he picked up his peezletree stick in his hand, and he walked out Pharaoh's kitchen door, down the steps and down the hill to the cornfield, said, "Call in all the field hands! Dig up that big peezletree down there in the river bottom, wrap up its roots in a tow sack-ah, put it in one of them big Studebaker wagons, and hitch four big Missouri mules to it. Don't hitch none of them little ga'nt cornfield mules to that wagon, 'cause we aimin' to march out of Egypt wi' high heads!"

Bretheren and Sisteren, them Chil'ren of Israel all marched down that Red Sea road-ah, smack-dab in the middle of the morning, wi' red tassels on them mules' hames, and wi' a United States flag a-flying from the topmost limb of that peezletree, and the Lord Hisse'f a-smilin' down on that whole teetotal procession!

But now when they got down to the Red Sea, them Chil'ren looked around, and they said, "Moses, we don't see no ferry, and we don't see no boat-ah. How we a-goin' to get across this here sea? Jus' look at the fix you and the Lord got us in here-ah!"

But Moses, he was jus' as cool as the center seed of a cucumber. He wove that peezletree stick seb'n times from the east to the west, and the wind blowed throughout the leaves of that peezletree, and blowed the Red Sea back! And the Chil'ren of Israel marched across on dry feet-ah! But when they got to the other side, they looked back and seen the hordes of Egypt a-comin', and the Chil'ren of Israel got scared-ah! They huddled 'round Moses like sheep 'round a shepherd-boy, but Moses, he wud't scared. He jus' turned 'round and wove his peezletree stick seb'n times from the west to the east, and the wind blowed back through the leaves of that peezletree and drownded all the hordes of Egypt-ah!

Forty days and forty nights the Chil'ren of Israel, they wandered in the wilderness, probably cane brakes and laurel hells. One mornin' Moses woke up and went down to the mule lot and saw the mules ain't been curried, and the peezletree ain't been watered, and Moses he tongue-whipped the stable boss for his sorry ways. And the Chil'ren of Israel, they complained to Moses, said, "We're hongry. We ain't had nothin' much in the way of vittles-ah." And Moses said, "Go on up there to the peezletree and eat peezles."

And Bretheren and Sisteren, they picked up twelve basketfulls of good ripe peezles! It's a fact that in sacred and profane history that it's recorded a good ripe peezle is better'n 'possum and sweet taters with brown gravy-ah! Now, some folks say that was manna they et there in the wilderness. 'T'warn't nothing 'tall but peezles-ah! Some folks say 't'was a pillar of fire by night and a pillar of clouds by day that led them out'n the wilderness. 'T'warn't nothing 'tall but the moonshine on the leaves of the peezletree by night and the sun on the peezletree in the daytime.

Bretheren and Sisteren, I say unto you verily, verily, in the last great day, when the angel Gabriel shall come-ah, and the earth is rolled up like an old newspaper and cast on the fiery flames of hell to burn, and the sheep is gathered on the right, and the goats gathered on the left, in that day Bretheren and Sisteren, what are you goin' to be, a sheep or a goat? In that day do you expect to take your place on the right and be told off by St. Peter as you march through them Pearly Gates-ah, and walk on them golden streets a-wearin' that white robe and them golden slippers-ah? Bretheren and Sisteren, I want you to be wearin' a right smart-sized bunch of peezle leaves pinned up here on your bosoms! Amen!

PREACHER DRY FRYE'S ORDINATION EXAMINATION

by the Reverend Patrick E. Napier
from Bowling Green, Kentucky

Everybody knows Old Dry Frey. He is a mountain preacher. You'll find his story in Richard Chase's *Grandfather Tales*, published by Houghton Mifflin back in 1948. After becoming an ordained Presbyterian minister, I became interested in just how Old Dry Frye became ordained, so I did a little research on the matter.

It seems that when Old Dry Frye was a young man, he felt the call to preach, so he attended an association meeting, said he'd been called to preach and asked to be forthwith examined. Straightway, the elders they begin to ask him questions:

"Can you write?"

"No, hain't much of a scribe, but I can make my mark."

"Can you read?"

"No, can't, but my wife, she reads powerful good, and she reads to me."

"Do you know the Bible?"

"Yes, I do. My wife, she's read it to me from kiver to kiver."

"What part of the Bible do you like best?"

"The New Testament."

"What book of the New Testament?"

"The Book of Parables."

"Which Book of Parables?"

"The Book of the Good Samaritan."

"All right then. Give us your interpretation of the Book of the Good Samaritan."

And so, Old Dry Frye began, "There was a man went down from Jerusalem to Jericho, and he fell among twelve spies who came up from Egypt with a bunch of people who had been lost for forty years. He fell among them spies and a couple of them beat him up and robbed him of thirty pieces of silver. He fell on hard ground and in a ditch, and the thorns grew up and choked him. He was bruised and afflicted, but he opened not his mouth.

"A preacher man in a long coat of many colors came along, and he said he'd help him out but that he'd married a wife and a yoke of oxen and could not come.

"Straightway, that feller got out of that ditch. He found a mule tied to a tree, and he got on and rode furiously. He run under a sycamore tree, and his hair got caught up in the limbs of that tree, which nearly jerked his head off, and there he was, hung between the ground and the earth.

"Straightway he looked up in that tree, which wasn't easy, and there was a little man up there. The man said, 'I will go call Delilah. She's a good hand to cut hair.' So, Delilah come over there and cut off his hair, and he fell into stony places and the thorns growed up and choked him. He was bruised and afflicted, but he opened not his mouth.

"And straightway it started to rain, and he got in a boat. He floated around for what seemed a thousand years but it was only forty days and forty nights, but it rained all the time. A raven and a dove fed him, and his hair growed back, so the first thing he did when he hit dry land was to push the pillars down from a big building.

"He figured that the whole world—or at least the holler he lived in—would be in tee-total flood. But the sun had stood still and dried up all the water, and there wasn't nothing but a valley of dry bones. When the dry bones started to rise up, he said 'I'm getting out of here for I must be about my father's business!' And he left there, and as he was going through Samaria, he met Lot's wife. She was a pillar of salt by day, but let me tell you, she was a ball of fire by night!

"Then he come to an inn and said, 'Behold I stand at the door and knock,' but the innkeeper said, 'I have no room in the inn, but let us kill the fatted calf and make a great feast.' But the man said, 'Let me first go and bury my father and compel him to come.' But when he went out into the highways and hedges, he saw Jezabel. She had been married seven times, and ever' one of them husbands died. Jezabel, she was putting on make-up because she heard that Jehu was a-coming. Jehu was in a swivet, though, and told them to throw her down, and they throwed her down seventy times seven, and they picked up twelve bushel baskets of the fragments for dog food. Now I ask you what in the world's going to happen to her in judgment? Whose wife will she be?

"After three days, he rose up and paid the price and went to Jericho but the wall had been tore down, so he went back to Jerusalem and went up on a mountain and built three sheds— one for Moses, one for Jonah, and one for hisself, so that they might dwell in the house of the Lord forever."

And that concluded Old Dry Frye's interpretation of the Book of the Good Samaritan.

There were no more questions, so one of the elders made a motion which was seconded, and passed unanimously that Mr. Dry Frye be ordained to preach.

COON SKIN HUNTIN'

The following story was collected by the late Dr. Leonard Roberts, Kentucky folklorist, from Charles Halcomb, Big Leatherwood, Kentucky, who had heard it on a '"talking machine" record when a boy. Roberts included it as No. 78a in his South from Hell-fer-Sartin: Kentucky Mountain Folk Tales *(Lexington: University of Kentucky Press, 1955), pp. 158-60. This type is called a scrambled tale, and several variants have been collected. It employs interesting folk speech, with archaic usage, such as "clumb" for "climbed." Used by permission of Edith Roberts.*

Now me and my paw we live down in Moonshine Holler about a mile, mile and a half, maybe two mile. The other day I told paw le's go a-larrapin, terrapin coon skin huntin' if he cared, so he asked me he didn't care. So we got out and called up all the dogs but ole Shorty—called him up, too. So we went on down the mountain till we got to the top of the hill and all the dogs treed one but ole Shorty, and he treed it too, up a long tall slim slick sycamore blackgum saplin', about ten feet above the top, right out on an ole dead chestnut snag. So I told paw I'd climb up and twist him out if he cared, so he asked me he didn't care. I clumb up and shook and shook and shook, and directly I heard something hit the ground. Looked around and it was me. Everyone of them doggoned ole dogs jumped on top of me, but ole Shorty, and he jumped on top of me too. Now when I come to my right mind I told paw to knock 'em off if he cared, and he asked me he didn't care. Then paw picked up a pine knot and knocked them all off but ole Shorty—knocked him off too.

So we decided that was enough huntin' for one day and started back down the hill and all the dogs holded one in a huckleberry log about two foot through at the little end. So I told paw we'd have to cut him out to save time if he cared and he asked me he didn't care. And paw picked up the ax, and the first lick he cut ole Shorty's long smooth tail off right behind his ears. Just like to ruint my dog. So we started back down the hill and paw seen all the punkins in the pig patch and we chased them doggoned punkins all over the field and finally I got mad and picked one up by the tail and slammed its brains out over a pig. Then paw he talked to me like I was a redheaded stepchild, be gosh!

So we laid up the gate and shut the fence and then paw told me to shuck and shell him a bucket o' slop. So I's settin' there shuckin' and shellin' that bucket o' slop and I decided to go down to Sal's house. She lives in Moonshine Holler on the tough of the creek and the furder you go the tougher it gits. Sal lives in the main last house. It's a big white house painted green, both front doors on the backside.

So I told paw I'd ride that day, it being kinda sunny, if he cared, and he asked me he didn't care. So I went out in the lot, put the bridle on the barn, the hoss on the saddle, led the fence upside the gate and the hoss got on. So we went ridin' along down the road, study like and all at once a stump in the corner of the hoss got scared and r'ared up and throwed me off right face fo'most, a-flat o' my back, in a gully about ten feet deep, right in a briar patch. Tore one sleeve outten my Sunday britches. So I got up an 'peared to be like I wa'n't hurt. Brushed off the hoss and went leadin' him on down the road.

Got to Sal's house and she had both front doors shut wide open and the winders nailed down. So I knowed she was glad to see me. So I hitched the fence to the hoss and went in and throwed my ole hat in the fireplace and spit on the bed and down I sit in a big armchair on a stool. So we begin to talk about pat and polly-cake and all other kind o' cake, and finally Sal 'lowed, "Bud, le's go down in the peach orchard and get some apples and make a huckleberry pie for dinner." So I asked her I didn't care. And we went down to the peach orchard, and I was just as close to Sal as I could get, me one side of the road and her on the oth-er'n. So we got down to the peach orchard and I told Sal I'd climb up the pear tree and shake off some apples if she didn't care. And she asked me she didn't care. And so I clumb up and shook and shook and shook till the limb I was standin' on broke off and throwed me right a-straddle of a barbwire fence, both feet on the same side. Broke my right shin just above my left ole elbow. And so I told Sal right then and there that'd be the last time in the Moonshine Hollow, and I hain't been back since, be gosh!

GOD BLESS THE PEOPLE OF ESTILL COUNTY

Thomas D. Clark, historian laureate of Kentucky, noted several backwoods orators in his The Rampaging Frontier *(New York: Bobbs-Merrill, 1939), one being a certain Representative Mullins from Estill County, Kentucky (pp. 134-35). Professor Clark's presentation of the Honorable Mullins and his speech is used here with his permission:*

One such "honorable representative," Mullins by name, floated into Frankfort on the famous old Kentucky River packet, the Blue Wing, and began "looking into the situation" at once. At court day back in his beloved county, following adjournment of the assembly, he gave an accounting of his lawmaking activities in a sonorous oration which fell a little short of the manner of Clay. "Feller Citizens!" saluted a red-faced Honorable Mullins, "when you elected me to the legislature I wished I mought have a tallest pine growed in the mountings, so that I mought strip the limbs from the same and make it into an enormous pen, and dip it in the waters of the Kaintuck River and write acrost the clouds, 'God bless the people of Estill county!'

"Arter you elected me I went down to Frankfort on the Blue Wing and as we wended our winding sinuosities amidst its labyrinthian meanderings, the birdlets, the batlets, and the owlets flew outen their secret hidin' places and cried out to me in loud voices: 'Sail on, Mullins, thou proud defender of thy country's liberties.'

"When I reached Frankfort, I went up into the legislatur hall and thar I spied many purty perlicues a-hangin on the ceiling to pay for which you had been shamefully robbed of by unjest taxation. When matters of small importance were before the body I lay like a bull pup a-baskin in the sunshine, with a blue-bottled fly a ticklin of my nose; but when matters of great importance come up, I riz from my seat, like the Numidian lion of the desert, shuck the dew drops from my mane, and gave three shrill shrieks for liberty!"

The following story also illustrates an adroit use of the language. It is among the papers of D.K. Wilgus, the late folklorist, donated to Special Collections at the Hutchins Library of Berea College by Dr. Eleanor Long-Wilgus.

"BLACK" SHADE COMBS

by Josiah H. Combs

"Black" Shade Combs was a picturesque mountaineer, whose long black beard descending swept his rugged breast. "Black" was merely a pseudonym, for Shade was white, with no great claim to education and culture, but blessed with native wit and intelligence. Shade and some other mountaineers found themselves in Frankfort, stopping at the Capitol Hotel, frequented by Senators and Representatives, and by the elite. It was dinner time. Directly across from Shade sat an elegantly dressed woman, of easy morals and notorious reputation. A waiter came to the table to take the orders. He addressed the courtesan:

Waiter: "What will you have, Lady?"

Courteson: "First bring me a thimbleful of honeyed and spiced nectar, as sweet and soothing as an infant's cordial; second, bring me a tiny bowl of potage, seasoned with mushrooms and nightingale tongues; third, bring me a modest portion of asparagus tips, gently smothered with vinaigrette sauce; fourth, bring me a small beefsteak as tender as a chicken's breast; fifth, bring me a soft silk napkin to spread upon my bosom—and please inform me who this gentleman is that sits opposite me."

"Black" Shade was thinking, and thinking fast. He drank in the whole import of the woman's obvious satire and contempt. By the time the waiter got around to him he was ready with a retort stinging and terrible:

Waiter: "And what will you have, Sir?"

"Black" Shade: "First, fetch me a pint of moonshine liquor as clear as crystal and as strong as hell; second, fetch me a big bowl of onion soup full of hog kidneys and 'mountain oysters'; third, fetch me a bowl of hominy swimmin' in hog grease; fourth, fetch me a hunk of beefsteak as tough as a saddleskirt; fifth, fetch me a burlap sack to spread over my hairy breast—and (pointing straight at the woman of easy morals opposite him) please inform me who that God damned chippy is that sits opposite me."

THE HIGH CONSTABLE'S WARRANT

Here is another piece from Josiah H. Combs. Combs was one of the first graduates of the Hindman Settlement School and went on to graduate from Transylvania University and to earn a doctorate in languages from the Sorbonne. He was a lifelong student of Appalachian humor, speech and folksongs. He introduces here a story showing a mighty effort at communicating the authority of the law.

The cold and unemotional language of the law may sometimes be couched in terse and expressive diction in Highland warrants and indictments. More than a hundred years ago, in the state of Jett's Creek, "Bloody" Breathitt County, a "hi official magistrat" issued such a writ. And this is how one Jackson Terry authorized one Miles Terry to go "Forthwith and forthcomin" for the apprehension of one Henderson Harris of said county:

I, Jackson Terry hi official, magistrat, squir and justice of pece, do hereby issu the following rit against Henderson Harris, charging him with assalt and the battery and the brech of the pece, on his brutherin law, Tom Fox by name.

This warnt cuses him of kicking, bitin' and scratchin' and throin rocks and doing everything that was mean and contrary to the law in the State of Jetts Creek aforesaid.

This warent otherises the hy constable, Miles Terry by name, to go forthright and forthcomin and arest the sed Henderson Harris and bring him too bee delt with accordin to the law of Jetts Creek and aforesaid.

This warent otherises the hy constable to tak him wher he finds him on the hill side as well as in the level, to tak him wher he aint as well as wher he is and bring to bee delt with accordin to the laws of Jetts Creek aforesaid,

> *Jinary 2d, 1838*
> *Jackson Terry, magistrat and squir and justice pece of*
> *State of Jetts Creek aforesaid.*

JUDGE PATTON

Following are examples of the rhetoric and wit of the famous anti-bellum Judge Patton of eastern Kentucky. The first version is by John Ed McConnell and is used by permission from his book, A Compendium of Kentucky Humor *(1987). The second is from Josiah H. Combs, whose stories appear elsewhere in the this book.*

Those Rotten Horse Hitchers

The account that follows was given me by my wife's uncle, Dr. Fred Millard, a dentist in Mt. Sterling, Kentucky.

Judge Patton, from Johnson County, Kentucky, in his charge to a grand jury said, "The beautiful little hamlet of Paintsville, situated on the placid waters of the Big Sandy, beautified and made more lovely by the good hands of our fair ladies, wherein they planted shade trees where men might find rest and the birds might build their nests unmolested in the shade thereof.

"Some among us would defile this city by hitching horses to the trees where they would gnaw the bark, paw the roots and kill those trees. Indict them, damn them. We'll teach them how to hitch their horses. Some of those men would ride a jackass into the Garden of Eden and hitch them to the Tree of Life, if they were allowed to.

"Go with me if you will, in an afternoon of leisure time, into the countryside about. As we travel about along we would meet a man coming in on a flea-bitten gray nag with a red tassel in its bridle and a bright red rose in the lapel of his coat, singing, 'The Last Gold Dollar is Gone.' Indict him too, damn him. We'll teach him how to take care of his money.

"As we traverse the countryside, we would follow various characters. We would go along perhaps and meet a man with overalls. He … carries an old muzzle loading rifle, a squirrel hung to his suspender buckle. You don't want to molest that man, he might have a sick wife or invalid mother and he would help provide for their welfare but as you proceed a little farther along to the mouth of the hollow, you'll find a guy sitting on a stump picking a banjo, singing, 'Hello My Little Love,' and a man walking along with a Winchester rifle on his arm. You ask him, 'What are you doing?' 'Oh, I'm just knocking around.' Indict them! For dead sure they're up to no good!"

John Ed McConnell

BANJER PICKERS

Judge Patton, whose circuit lay deep in the Highlands, once instructed the grand jury:

"Gentlemen of the Jury! Whenever there slinks into this com-

munity one of them rovin', shiftless, 'Sourwood Mountain' ban-
jer-pickers, watch him; watch him as he sits on a rock by the side
of the road at the mouth of some holler, a slouch hat pulled
down over his eyes, wearing a blue celluloid collar, a red bandan-
ner handkercher around his neck, a banjer strung across his
bosom, a-smellin' of cinnamon oil, and a-pickin' of 'Sourwood
Mountain'—fine that man, gentlemen, fine him! For if he ain't
already done something, he's a-goin' to. Gentlemen! every time I
see one of them characters come into my community, I go
straight home to my daughter."

Dr. Josiah H. Combs

THE BELLE OF BLAND

Nanny Belle Robinette was twenty-five years old in 1927 and
well-known locally as "The Belle of Bland" (Bland County,
Virginia). With her long flowing red hair tied in a ponytail she
was driving her new-fangled Gardner Touring car down one of
those old country roads and speeding, of course (which was nor-
mal for her), when all of a sudden on a stiff curve she met a
policeman in a twenty-six Dodge. They almost collided—he had
to swerve sharply to avoid her hitting him. As soon as he could
find a wide place in the road so that he could turn around, he
gave chase.

He ate a lot of her dust before she turned into a filling station, jumped out of her car and ran quickly into the restroom
and slammed the door. The big old stony-faced policeman got
out of his car, put one foot on the bumper and in a comfortable
position simply waited for her to come out. A small but excited
crowd gathered. They knew that "the Belle of Bland" was in
trouble! After about five minutes she came out buttoning her
dress. She sidled up to the policeman, looked him square in the
eye in a smart-alec and flirty sort of way, and said, "Ha!—You

didn't think I would make it, did you?"

The crowd was shocked. The policeman was shocked too. The crowd began to sniggle and giggle. According to one eye witness, the policeman's face turned as "red as 'ary a beet" you have ever seen. Nanny Belle simply twisted over to her car and sped away.

Jesse Ball
BLUEFIELD, WEST VIRGINIA

THE DEAF BUT NOT DUMB PLOUGHMAN

by Chet Atkins
as told to Billy Edd Wheeler

When I was young not too many people were impressed with my guitar playing in Luttrell, Tennessee, the little mountain town near Knoxville where I was born and partly raised.

But one man believed in me who couldn't even hear my guitar playing. His name was Azro Thomas, a big mountain man who was deaf and dumb. Azro told me many times, in his awkward way of making gutteral sounds to accompany his sign language, "You'll have money here ... and here," touching his shirt pockets and his front pants pockets with his big rough hands.

When Azro plowed he had a special language his horse understood perfectly. He yelled, "Fog-ogg!" when he wanted the horse to get up and "Poooh!" when he wanted the horse to stop.

Once my brother Lowell played a trick on Azro.

Lowell went to the garden patch on the side of the mountain where Azro was plowing and hid in the bushes. After Azro got hitched up he trailed the reins back, took hold of the plow, and yelled, "Fog-ogg!" The horse started out. Then from the bushes Lowell yelled, "Poooh!" and the horse stopped. Azro stared in surprise. He yelled "Fog-ogg!" again and the horse lunged forward, but stopped immediately as Lowell yelled "Poooh!" from the bushes.

Azro was dumbfounded. He was also irritated at this dumb horse. He yelled "Fog-ogg!" and when the horse stopped at Lowell's command he dashed forward, shook the horse's head roughly, pounded it once between the eyes, and unleashed a series of gutteral expletives so hot they withered the outer leaves of the trees at the edge of the garden patch. And the poor horse was so agitated and confused he almost jumped out of the harness when Lowell yelled "Fog-ogg!" as Azro was walking back to pick up the handles of the plow.

Azro missed his grab.

The horse was off to the races. He dashed away in a zigzag across the furrows, across a grassy buffer area, into an adjoining field where young corn was already coming up about knee-high. He trampled a fair percentage of it down and slashed the field with several fresh gashes before the point of the plow dug in deep behind a rock, jolting the horse to a shuddering halt, causing it to lose its feet and land hard on its hind quarters.

The horse sat there for a moment, as if trying to figure it all out, which Azro had already done. He was deaf but he was no dummy. As he approached the horse he cast his eyes back to the bushes, thinking that if there were a jokester there he might take this opportunity to get away. Which, of course, is what Lowell had in mind. But Azro saw him sneaking away through the bushes and took off after him like a hound after a rabbit.

He chased Lowell up and down the hollers and mountainsides for who-stayed-the-longest, and I do believe he would've killed him if he'd caught up with him.

But he didn't.

And my brother died a natural death.

I went back to Luttrell not too long ago and went to see Azro, who was quite old and starting to go a little blind. They didn't think he would recognize me but when I approached him and got up close to his face and said, "Azro, do you know who I am?" he got a small glint of recognition in his eyes, like a man waking up from a pleasant dream, smiled, and made a gesture with his hands like a man playing a guitar.

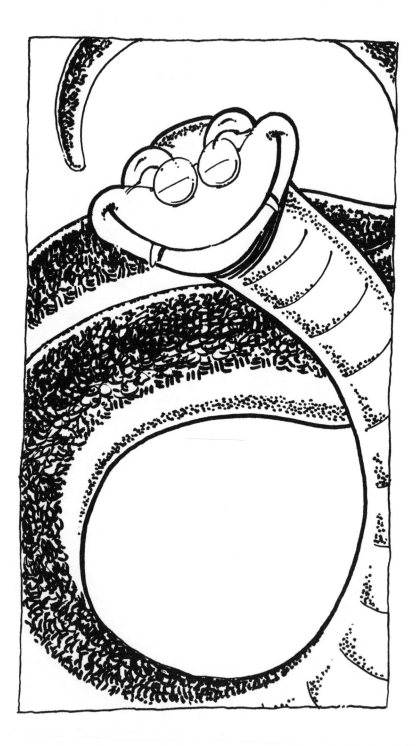

The Laughing Snake:
A Serpentine Look at Appalachian Humor

by Jim Wayne Miller

Delivered at the 4th Festival of Appalachian Humor
Berea College, Berea, Kentucky, July 1993

Analyzing humor is almost predictably self-defeating. The essayist E.B. White said analyzing humor "is like dissecting a frog. Few people are interested and the frog dies of it."

Humor and analysis go at things in altogether different ways. Humor puts things together—in surprising and unexpected ways. Analysis takes things apart—through rather routine procedures. And this difference is the heart of the problem.

If you think treatises on humor are funny, think again. To bone up for this festival, I read some books, and re-read some others. I started out with William Hazlitt's 19th century *Lectures on the Comic Writers, Etc., of Great Britain,* thinking I would laugh my way through them. I hadn't got halfway through the first lecture, "On Wit and Humor," before I found myself thinking: I guess you had to be there. Then I re-read Sigmund Freud's monumental analysis, *Wit and Its Relation to the Unconscious*—with a growing realization that I had completely repressed my first reading of it.

Humor is a deep subject. I get dizzy looking down into it. Even the simplest questions prove tough to answer. Why is it, for instance, that we laugh when somebody else tickles us but we don't laugh when we tickle ourselves? Think about that.

Somebody put this question to a bunch of smart people at the British Broadcasting System, a BBC Brain Trust. They hemmed and hawed and giggled for a long time and finally decided the question was "one of the insoluble mysteries of human nature," to quote Arthur Koestler, from his book *The Act of Creation* (Macmillan, 1964).

I agree with just about everything my predecessors at this festival have said when they've taken a thoughtful look at humor. I'm with Billy Edd Wheeler when he says "it's either funny or it ain't" in his book (with Loyal Jones), *Laughter in Appalachia* (August House, 1987). I'd go further and say humor is a lot like obscenity: I may not be able to define it, but I know it when I see it—or hear it.

I heartily agree with Dr. W. Gordon Ross that "unthreatening ugliness and playful frustration" are sources of humor, as when we cause a baby to laugh by making an ugly face or holding something out to the child and then, when the child reaches for it, pulling it back. Dr. Ross is right, too, I think, to say that when humor stops being playful and becomes derisive and scornful, it stops being humor and becomes something else.

I think there's no doubt, as Bill Lightfoot maintains, that jokes have a psychological dimension: they often gratify the teller in some way (*Curing the Cross-Eyed Mule*, August House, 1989). Sometimes jokes gratify a whole group, and so are funny to members of one group but not to other people. Brier jokes and Buckeye jokes are of this insider/outsider type. Brier's wife had twins. Brier got his gun, went out looking for the other feller.— That gratifies Buckeyes. Buckeye was down in Kentucky, walking out in a field. Came to a ditch full of plastic milk jugs. Thought he'd found a cow's nest.—That gratifies Briers.

Jack Higgs is surely right when he points out that tricks are a source of humor because "Tricks are the essence of Nature" (*Laughter in Appalachia*, August House, 1987). There is often a suddenness about humor. The surprise, the twist, is the essence of this joke, analyzed by Sigmund Freud: "The Prince, travelling through his domains, noticed a man in the cheering crowd who bore a striking resemblance to himself. He beckoned him over and asked: 'Was your mother ever employed in my palace?' 'No, Sire,' the man replied, 'but my father was.'" (Koestler)

We are set up to study humor seriously and methodically nowadays. There's an International Society for Humor Studies that has conferences scheduled through 1995 in Luxembourg; Ithaca, New York; and Birmingham, England. (Its unpronounceable acronym is ISHS, which is sort of funny in itself.) A prominent member of ISHS brought out this year a weighty volume which, in ten chapters, deals with every kind of humor I'm sure the author could think of—parody, paradox, puns, nonsense, black, and sick humor. (Can sick humor be medicinal?) And there's a lot in the book about humor as therapy, medicine, and physiology. (Don L. F. Nilsen, *Humor Scholarship: A Research Bibliography*, Greenwood, 1993).

Laughers Are Problem Solvers

A new publication, *The Journal of Jocular Nursing*, claims to "take a fresh look at the field of nursing by poking fun at it." The journal mounted a convention in St. Louis in June, 1993. One of the conference participants, Dr. Clifford Kuhn, a professor of psychiatry at the University of Louisville School of Medicine, prescribes thirty minutes of laughter per day for his patients, and may fill as well as write his prescriptions, for the story says he is, in addition to being a psychiatrist, a stand-up comedian.

Kuhn has interesting things to say about humor and laughter. Only in the last two hundred years in Western society, he says, has laughter in public been condoned. "It used to be viewed as we might view belching." On humor and physiology, Kuhn says that "twenty seconds of hearty laughter ... doubles the heart rate and keeps it elevated for five minutes ... Laughter also stimulates the immune system and increases tolerance for pain in both the short and long term ..." Besides that, "laughers are better problem solvers and tend to work better with others."

Well, yes. Yes to all these fine people and their views on humor. We can talk about humor as a separate thing, but it's always turning out to be more than any of our separate views of it. Arthur Koestler begins a book entitled *The Act of Creation* with a detailed examination of laughter and humor called "The Art of Discovery and the Discoveries of Art." Koestler sees everything that makes humor what it is as part of a pattern of central importance to all discovery, problem-solving, and creativity.

A person who can see a joke is also likely to be someone who can solve the problem. "The creative act of the humorist," Koestler says, "[brings about] a momentary fusion between two habitually incompatible matrices. Scientific discovery ... can be described in very similar terms ... Comic discovery is paradox stated—scientific discovery is paradox resolved."

I would add that the creative act of the humorist and the scientist also resembles that of the poet, who, when creating a metaphor, fuses "two habitually incompatible matrices," as when Carl Sandburg says "The past is a bucket of ashes," or when the psalmist says, "The Lord is my shepherd," or, for that matter, when I say, "Teaching is running in place with weights on your feet."

A classics professor and a gag writer at Berea College suggests what comic discovery and scientific discovery (or problem-solving) have in common. Professor Scott Emmons says humor is "a matter of trying to look at things differently. So is problem-solving ... You have to take ordinary things and play off them in a different situation that is still familiar." Yes. And the operative word is "play." There's a playfulness not only in humor, but in all problem-solving, scientific discovery, and even in "serious" poetry.

Feeling the Elephant Blind

Everybody I've mentioned here is right about humor, its essence and function. Because humor is all the things these people have said it is, does all the things they've said it does. But we're all like the blind sages who approach the elephant, feel one part of it, and then give a description. Humor is an animal each of us understands according to our own lights, or lack of lights. But it may not be the animal we think it is.

Actually, I'm all for studying humor—for going up to the animal again and again, feeling of it, and reporting back.

One of my favorite analysts of humor who works both sides of the street, who's both funny and thoughtful about being funny, is Loyal Jones. He knows that what people find funny and laugh at tells a lot about them. He says, for instance, that there are more jokes about religion in Appalachian humor than any other subject. That tells us something about Appalachia. I suspect it has something to do with the fact that we're fundamentally Calvinists, regardless of our church affiliation. This means we know we're all fallen, fallible, and there's nothing so base or mean or low-down we're not capable of. We're sinners. But, when we take one another one at a time, we find some mighty fine people, like Henry Vaughan, Cratis Williams' mentor, who was, Williams said, "a better man than I ever wanted to be."

The "Yaller Jacket" Congregation

One of my favorite quips about religion in Appalachia involves the outsider in a community who notices two churches right across the road from each other, one freshly painted and well-maintained, the other looking as if it had been abandoned. The visitor inquires about the unused church. A local whittler informs him that the church's congregation is "like yaller jackets. They die out in the winter and recruit up again in the summer."

Jones notes, too, that there are a lot of rube/city slicker jokes in Appalachian humor, an old theme in American humor generally. I like the one about the two city slickers out in the country dying for a drink of water. They see this old woman bringing a bucket of water from her spring with the drinking gourd floating in the bucket. They ask for a drink. She says, "Shore." They notice then that she's dirty, snaggle-toothed, and has a big dip of snuff in her mouth. They want a drink bad, but the thought of drinking from that gourd just about gags them. So, when the first one drinks, he turns the gourd upside down and drinks from the hole in the handle. The old woman watches, says, "I declare, you're the first man I ever saw that drinks water out of a gourd just the way I do!"

Rubeism is a relative matter, as is illustrated by this story from James Still's *Wolfpen Notebooks*:

> Old Sid Pridemore never went nowhere much in his life. Never traveled farther than the forks of Troublesome Creek to pay his taxes, and to set once on a jury. That was yonder when the creekbed was the road and you had to travel by horseback, by wagon or shanks-mare.
>
> When final-last a road was built up Quicksand and an automobile could get in and out, Sid's son-in-law, John Zeek Smith, talked him into going with him to Hazard in Perry County. Going to let Sid see a speck of the world.
>
> Well, sir, they got to Hazard and old Sid's eyes were big as turnips. He kept saying, "What's creation come to?" John Zeek drove into Hazard and was heading down the main street when he suddenly mashed on the brake and came to a full stop. Old Sid, he asked, "What are ye quitting for?" And John Zeek he said, "Don't you see that red light hanging overhead?" Old Sid said, "Why, go right on. We'll miss it fully ten feet." (This and other material reprinted from James Still, *The Wolfpen Notebooks*, University Press of Kentucky, ©1991, by permission of the publishers.)

Humor is hard to analyze because it can walk and chew gum at the same time. Humor can rub its belly and pat itself on the head at the same time. Humor has a lot of irons in the fire. It is and does several things at once.

Henri Bergson developed an entire theory of laughter on the distinction between man and the machine, or what he calls "the mechanical encrusted in the living." Our necessary dependence on physical laws, despite our positions of honor and dignity, can be funny. The absent-minded professor who boils his watch while holding an egg in his hand. Hamlet getting hiccoughs. Such situations, says Koestler, "deflate the victim's dignity, intellect, or conceit by demonstrating his dependence on coarse bodily functions and physical laws." Like James Still writing about the widow bent on re-marrying:

> She was a widow, and he a widow-man. She was so deaf she couldn't hear herself poot. Well, I worked it up for them to meet, for they both wanted to be married in a bad way. I brought them together and they didn't know how to start talking to each other. Finally he asked, "What time is it?" And she said quick, "Yes!"

Or the drunk:

> He was in bed drunk, and a cat crawled under the covers and had a gang of kittens. He thought he felt something funny and he runs his hand down to feel, and he hallooed to his woman, "Hey, Liz, come quick. My belly has busted and my insides are running out."

Or this one told once by Byron Crawford, who writes a column for the *Louisville Courier-Journal*:

> This old farmer dearly loved Coca-Colas but was too stingy to buy them. The loafers at the country store knew this, so when the farmer came to the store they'd tease him a while and then buy him a Coke. One blistering July day the farmer's wife sent him to the store for a ten-cent spool of white thread. By the time he got to the store the farmer was wringing wet with sweat, and thirsty. Oh, he was thirsty! He looked so dry the loafers at the store felt sorry for him. "Uncle Billy," one of them said, "you do look hot, and you must be thirsty. Here, let me buy you an ice-cold Co-cola." To which the old man replied: "If it's all the same to you, I'd sooner have a spool of white thread."
>
> Reduced to being one thing, we're funny.

Staples of Appalachian Humor

Lots of jokes and anecdotes generate a twist or unexpected turn out of the consistency of life. An anecdote about Zebulon

Vance, the Civil War governor of North Carolina, shows that sometimes the expected is unexpected.

When Vance was a boy, he was, as we would say, awful bad to cuss, even at school, and his teacher tried to break him of the habit. According to Richard Walser, in his book *Tarheel Laughter* (University of North Carolina Press, 1974), the teacher had Vance sit over in a corner of the classroom at a mouse-hole, "with a pair of tongs in his hands, and told him not to open his mouth until he caught the mouse. Zeb took his place at the hole, and the work of the school went on. Finally the time for 'spelling by heart' came round, and in the excitement of the contest everybody forgot about Zeb. All at once he startled the school by shouting out: 'Damned if I haven't got him!' And, sure enough, he had the mouse gripped with the tongs."

These twists and unexpected turns that are, paradoxically, the result of perfect consistency may be classified as a variant of the trick that is simply in the nature of things. And the trick, or rusty, is a staple of Appalachian humor. It has been with us from pioneer and settlement days, illustrated by Davy Crockett's story of selling the storekeeper the same coonskin half a dozen times. Donald Davidson characterizes our humor well in this passage from his *The Tennessee* (Rinehart, 1946):

> From the companies of loungers who whittled and spat beneath the shade trees of the square, the rollicking satirical humor jostled upward into the courtroom and nudged its way into the proceedings of legislatures. No matter how great a man's dignity, he could not always be standing on dignity alone. If you could not take a joke, you must not expect people to take you seriously. The people made laws, but what could be funnier than laws and lawmaking? The people were religious, but what was more ridiculous than doctrinal disputes?

Common Sense vs. Book Learning

There was (and still is) an anti-intellectual, anti-establishment element in our religious and political humor, a determination to level the high and mighty, to turn everything topsy-turvy, to make the last first, and the first last. It's a humor that favors the underdog, and deeds over words. Character is what we are in the dark—or what we are when stripped of our credentials, our societally defined status, our resumes and degrees, our positions of authority and dignity.

Davidson illustrates this humor with an anecdote from James K. Polk's race for governor of Tennessee:

> Polk was artful and able, a great stump speaker without peer in public debate. Against the unbeatable Polk the Whigs put up a curious figure, James C. Jones—commonly known as "Lean Jimmy" Jones. Polk was small of stature, dapper, and elegant. Jones was six feet two and weighed only 125 pounds. He had an enormous nose, a wide slit of a mouth, and the deceptively solemn countenance of the backwoods humorist. The audience began to roar as soon as he stalked to the front of the platform. To Polk's elaborate argument, made in the classic style, Jones attempted no direct reply, but ran his bony finger gently over a coonskin that he displayed to the audience and said, "Did you ever see such fine fur?" Jones was elected.

Lean Jimmy Jones might well have been the model for George Washington Harris's gangly, east Tennessee trickster, Sut Lovingood, who shows hostility to all established authority, respectability and dignity, despises sheriffs and circuit-riding preachers, and stylishly dressed encyclopedia salesmen. Sut cannot or will not even say the word "encyclopedia," and refers to the salesmen as "Onsightly Peter."

Sut deliberately bolts a horse at Mrs. Yardley's quilting party. The horse runs through the yard where several quilts are hanging on lines, gets a quilt over its head, rears, wheels, tears down all the quilts, and when Mrs. Yardley comes out of her house to see what's wrong, the horse tramples and kills her.

Sut is the quintessential trickster, with antecedents in the medieval German Till Eulenspiegel, a smart young peasant who pulls pranks on dukes, duchesses, magistrates and supposedly sophisticated but gullible townspeople.

And Sut's words are consistent with his deeds. Here is his summing up of the way things are generally:

> Whar thar ain't enuf feed, big childer roots littil childer outen the troff, an' gobbils up thar part. Jis' so the yeath over: bishops eats elders, elders eats common peopil; they eats sich cattil es me, I eats possums, possums eats chickins, chickins swallers wums, an' wums am content tu eat dus, an' dus am the aind ove hit all.

Sut has done here to social hierarchy what the bolting horse did to the decorum of Mrs. Yardley's quilting party. Sut's view turns the established social order upside down; it inverts the hierarchy of the Great Chain of Being. It is an elaborate verbal version of tipping over the neighbor's outhouse on Halloween. Sut tips over the entire philosophical and theological establishment.

There's something exhilarating about destruction and devastation. Children take about as much pleasure in tearing down a snowman as they did in making it. And, as adults, aren't we still capable of that elation we felt as children when we looked out the window, saw snow falling, and hoped the snow would fall six feet deep so there'd be no school next day? The storm may bring inconvenience, discomfort, even danger, but it also brings excitement through the suspension of routine and regulation. My mother didn't enjoy going to church as much after the order of worship was made available on a printed program. That made a routine out of the service, whereas before, you never knew what might happen next! We like a little disorder, even mischief.

Frontier Humor Lives On Today

Our contemporary Appalachian writers carry on the tradition of frontier humor embodied in the trickster Sut Lovingood. Sut illustrates the same kind of mischief that James Still observes in his neighbors in Knott County, and that he has used in his novel *River of Earth* (where Uncle Jolly starts a fire at the Kentucky state prison and then has his sentence commuted by the governor for putting it out), and in stories such as "A Ride on the Short Dog" and "The Run for the Elbertas." Still records one such prank in *The Wolfpen Notebooks:*

> "Monroe Lucas, he sent off to Montgomery Ward way back yonder and ordered a book on how to throw a voice. He learnt to do it, and he had a lot of big fun out of it. They say he was working in the coal mine once with a partner and the partner got mad about something and throwed his shovel down hard on the ground and the shovel spoke up and says, 'Hain't you ashamed treating me like a dog after I've helped you make bread for your family and raise your children?' That shook the partner up and he wasn't mad any more, and he picked up the shovel and says to it, 'You're the best friend I've got.'"

Sometimes the trick is one we unwittingly play on ourselves. In a widely told story (Cormac McCarthy has one version in his novel, *Child of God*), a fellow gets into a boxing match with a gorilla at a carnival. If he stays in the ring with the gorilla for three minutes, he wins fifty dollars. But more than prize money is at stake, for his cronies and a girlfriend are watching. Full of confidence, the challenger shows the gorilla some fancy footwork, then strikes the first blow. The gorilla seems indifferent. So the fellow hits the gorilla again. The gorilla's head snaps back, its eyes roll, as if dazed. Emboldened now, the prize money as good as spent, the fellow moves in for the finish. Just as he is about to hit the gorilla a third time, the animal jumps on his head, puts its foot in his mouth, and holds the fellow, speechless and humiliated, until attendants pull it off.

The anti-hero of that story is a direct descendent of Sut Lovingood. We're no different from other animals, Sut suggests when he says "bishops eats elders, elders eats common peopil," etc. Sut suffers humiliation at the Yardley quilting party when Mr. Yardley lodges his brogan in Sut's coattail, kicking him through the yard gate, rendering Sut numb from above his kidneys to his knees.

Sometimes nature plays the trick by sending a flood, blizzard, tornado, or hurricane. Our frontier humor revels in the description and exaggeration to tall-tale proportions of such natural phenomena, as in Fred Chappell's poem "My Father's

Hurricane":

> The sky was filled with flocks of roofs, dozens
> Of them like squadrons of pilotless airplanes,
> Sometimes so many you couldn't even see between.
> Little outhouse roofs and roofs of sheds
> And great long roofs of tobacco warehouses,
> Church steeples plunging along like V-2 rockets,
> And hats, toupees, lampshades, and greenhouse roofs.
> It [the hurricane] even blew your aunt's glass eyeball out.
> It blew the lid off a jar of pickles we'd
> Been trying to unscrew for fifteen years.

Where's a Bible When You Need One?

As in the case of Sut Lovingood at Mrs. Yardley's quilting, where the mischief gets out of hand and Mrs. Yardley is killed, or in James Still's "A Ride on the Short Dog," where Goady Spurlock's pranking results in his death, the humor can be grim. Maybe death, accident, and disaster ought not be funny, but they can be. Lynwood Montell relates this incident in his oral history, *Killings: Folk Justice in the Upper South* (University Press of Kentucky, 1986, by permission of the publishers):

> A man named Robert staggers home after a knife fight, bleeding to death. He remembered there was a verse in the Bible that stopped bleeding. Ezekiel 16:6, or something like that. He tells his wife to fetch the Bible. She says, "Why, Robert, they ain't a Bible on the place!" Robert says: "I've told you and told you to get one."
>
> "Well," his wife says, "we never did need one till right now."

I think that story is grimly funny because of the incongruity between the man's extremity and the ordinariness of the domestic bickering. There is grim humor also in a quip Jonathan Williams attributes to the novelist Cormac McCarthy, in his book, *In the Azure, Over the Squalor*. Speculating on somebody's whereabouts, McCarthy says: "He may be dead; or, he may be teaching English."

The Humor of Innocence
(or Wrecks on the Road of Communication)

There's a category of humor which, if somebody hasn't already identified it, I'd like to suggest: it's the humor that arises from innocence, usually the innocence of children or anyone, regardless of age, possessed of child-like innocence, like Jack in the Jack Tales. A visitor standing in the yard at a mountain home asks a little girl about a recent addition to the family: "Was it a boy?"

"Yes," the little girl replies, and then adds: "And it still is."

The humor arises from the discrepancy between what we know and what the child or child-like person knows, as in this entry from *I Thunk Me a Thaut* (Teacher's College Press, 1975), a diary Will McCall started keeping when his mother gave him a "ritin book" on his eighth birthday. An early entry concerns the marriage of Will's Uncle John:

> Uncul John and Nancy wuz hitched today. Atter supper I went down to see em. Door wuz locked. I nockd nockd nockd. No door. I nockd nockd nockd agin. No door. I knod they wuz home fur I cood heer em being still inside.

There's a later entry about Uncle John's bride Nancy and a conversation she has with Will's mother:

> When Nancy went to school she wuz good at books. Larned lots of jawbraker words. When ma asks her is it yit? Nancy sez, sez she, no I must be impregnible. I asked Nancy what impregnible meens. She says you will find out sum day. Hit makes me madurn all git out the way grownups keep saying that to me.
>
> Today in english class i asked teacher whut impregnible meens. He looked pins at me and sez, sez he, hits a durty word and ill whup you iffen I heer you speak hit agin. Must tell B bout that big word. We collect durty words and cuss words.

Much humor, it seems to me, arises from misunderstandings that result in wrecks on the road of communication, verbal versions of the havoc and mayhem Sut Lovingood looses at Mrs.

Yardley's quilting. Like the time somebody down at the store asked my father, "Have you read Jim's last book?"—And he said, "I hope so."

Or the time the young man knocked on a door in an affluent suburb and told the resident he was working his way through college doing odd-jobs for people. The resident, a busy man, did have a project he'd never got around to and he told the young man, "You can paint my porch. There's paint and brushes out in the garage." So the young man went to work and came back to the front door and collected his pay. As he was leaving, he said over his shoulder, "By the way, that's not a Porche, that's a Ferrari."

Tongue-and-Groove Cliches

Malapropisms are a variety of misunderstanding. People not on familiar terms with writing, and who get most of their information by ear only, often have to take a word or phrase by the scruff of the neck and jerk it into the realm of the familiar:

• Like the man I know in Bowling Green who heard on the radio about an earthquake somewhere that measured "six on the ricochet."

• And who, commenting on the cold cold spell we were having, said it was twenty below zero if you took into account the "windshield factor."

• Or the woman whose husband was in the "insensitive care unit" at the hospital.

• Or again the woman who told me that in school she never did learn to "diaphragm" sentences.

• Or the man in Newport, Tennessee, afraid he was about to go to jail, asked his lawyer if he couldn't "flea bargain."

• The preacher in Allen County, Kentucky, in the story of Jonah and the whale, told his congregation how the whale came up under Jonah and "engulped" him.

I've named a sub-variety of these verbal mishaps "tongue-and-groove" cliches. I heard a candidate for sheriff of Haywood County, North Carolina, declare in a radio ad run in the spring primary that his record "stood on itself." Here he fitted together two expressions, a political record that "speaks for itself," and the notion of "standing on your record"—just as the tongue fits into the groove of two pieces of flooring.

The tricks language plays on us probably ought to be understood as just another of nature's tricks. For in the same way that we're apt to slip on ice, or on the proverbial banana peel, we're apt to slip up anytime we open our mouths and speak, and have our intended meaning blown away like our hat in a gusting wind:

• For instance, Mrs. Reagan, defending the death penalty, once said: "I believe that people would be alive today if there were a death penalty."

• University of Louisville basketball coach Denny Crum once told an audience: "Most of our future lies ahead."

• And Yogi Berra, the Yankees catcher famous for such statements, told somebody: "Toots Shor's restaurant is so crowded nobody goes there anymore."

Some of our characteristic Appalachian humor comes from deliberately absurd statements, like these overheard and recorded by James Still in Knott County, Kentucky, and noted in his *Wolfpen Notebooks*:

• These shoes I'm wearing were so tight when I first bought them I had to wear them a while before I could put them on.

• He's got pretty good sense but he acts the fool so much you can't tell it.

• He's as slow as a schoolhouse clock.

• He's so slow it wouldn't hurt him to fall out of a tree.

• He wasn't born proper. Just sort of hatched out in the sun.

• These candidates don't miss a chance. They even work a funeral like a bee in a rosy-briar, shaking hands with everybody.

• You'd better shave before somebody steps on you for a wooly worm.

• When love comes to a rolling boil and can't be stirred down, it's time to get married.

• When you buy a pint of likker you're just buying a club to beat your brains out.

• Your garden is getting away from you. If you don't hoe it soon you'll have to buy a snake rake.

• What a girl! What a looker! Why, I could pick her up in my mouth like a kitten and carry her off.

• I'm off to see the prettiest girl who ever wore shoe leather and if I don't come back write me at Blue Eyes, Kentucky.

• On Groundhog Day the sun came out warm as wool.

These are examples of skillful, controlled use of language for intended effect. And it may be our "shrewd regard for essentials," as Horace Kephart says in *Our Southern Highlanders*, that generates such a striking number of Appalachian one-liners characterized by economy of speech. Such language delightfully blurs the boundary between humor and poetry. As does the language of Sam Creswell, auto mechanic, looking under the hood of Jonathan Williams' car:

> *your points is blue*
> *and your timing's*
> *a week off*

Or "Aunt Creasy, On Work," commenting on the reversal of traditional roles:

> *shucks*
> *I make the livin*
> *uncle*
> *just makes the livin*
> *worthwhile*

(Jonathan Williams, *Blues & Roots / Rue and Bluets*, Duke University Press, 1985)

Appalachian Humor:
As Unique as Churning Butter and as Universal as Getting Born

Can we say there is a distinctive Appalachian humor? Well, yes—and no. Our humor is like other aspects of our Appalachian history and culture, not altogether unique yet having distinguishing features. One of my students here at Berea spoke well to the question of Appalachian distinctiveness when she said: "We've never been similar enough to be the same [as other Americans], nor different enough to be separate."

So it is with our Appalachian speech, as Walt Wolfram points out in the *Appalachian Journal* (Spring 1984): there's not a feature of it that can't be found in the English of other times and places, but the features come together in southern Appalachia, like bits of colored glass in a kaleidoscope, in a configuration that renders our speech recognizably Appalachian. Wilma Dykeman said something similar about Appalachian literature when she wrote that Appalachian writing is "as unique as churning butter and as universal as getting born."

As with our language and literature, so with our humor. Our humor, like our language, is accented. There's not a feature of Appalachian humor that can't be found in the humor of other times, places, or groups. But the configuration of features, with an emphasis on frontier humor, renders it distinguishable. Appalachian humor, like Appalachian literature, is both unique and universal. Walt Whitman said of himself as a poet: I'm as bad as the worst but thank God I'm also as good as the best. We can say of Appalachian humor: it's as bad as the worst but also as good as the best. And our best humor, like the best humor of our greatest humorist, Mark Twain, offers us not an escape from reality but an escape from unreality.

I went through a stack of books trying to get a handle on humor, and finally came on something in James Still's *Wolfpen Notebooks* that reminded me of a story my grandpa told me down in Buncombe County years ago. He told me about this snake that bit his ax handle and the venom made the ax handle swell up into a log so big they hauled it off to the sawmill and made enough lumber to build a house. But when they painted the house, paint thinner or turpentine made the swelling go down. The house shrank until it looked like my sister's dollhouse, the boards no bigger than popsicle sticks.

What kind of snake was that? I asked my grandpa, for I'd

heard about coach-whip snakes, and horn snakes that had a stinger on their tail like a rooster's spur; hoop snakes that could put their tail in their mouth and come rolling after you; and glass snakes that could grow another tail if you cut theirs off, or grow back together if you cut them into pieces. What kind of snake could swell up a hoe handle like that? Grandpa never said.

Then, years later, I came on this in James Still's book: Sam Stamper, over in Knott County, told Still, "There's a serpent in this country we call the 'laughing snake.' If one ever bites you you'll laugh yourself to death. But I don't reckon one ever bit anybody." I thought: that's the snake! It was a laughing snake that bit my grandpa's hoe handle. For that's what humor does: it swells us up, then shrinks us down. Like that fellow that got in the ring with the ape, one minute feeling tree-top tall, thinking, "Well, well, how sweet it is." And the next minute has an ape on top of his head, its foot crammed in his jaw so he can't even holler for help.

Sam Stamper was right about there being a laughing snake in this country. But he was wrong when he said it never had bit anybody. It's bit just about everybody!

The Earliest Laugh in History

I didn't know it at the time but the laughing snake's bite explains the rollercoaster ride I took when I walked out past our barn that time with Selma. Selma lived down the road from us in Buncombe County, rode the same school bus, and she was growing up into a real blond-haired, blue-eyed looker. I thought a lot about Selma. One Saturday afternoon when everybody else was gone she came by the house—I think her mama had sent her after some rhubarb or something out of our garden. As we were walking out to the garden, there in the pasture below the barn, our bull served a heifer that was in season. My opportunity, I thought, to bring up a subject that had been much on my mind whenever I thought about Selma. I said, "I think it might be fun to do that." And Selma said, "Well, it's you-all's heifer." I never felt so small, so wrinkledy-shriveled.

A snake got us into trouble early on, there in the Garden of Eden. But some time after that we got bit by this other snake, the laughing snake, whose bite has been swelling and shriveling us ever since. When Abraham's wife Sarah was about ninety, and, as the Bible says, "it had ceased to be with her after the manner of women," she overheard God telling her husband Abraham that she was going to bear a child. Sarah laughed. That was one of the earliest recorded laughs, certainly.

But I believe there was an earlier laugh, and those scholars working with the Dead Sea Scrolls may turn it up yet. After Adam had eaten the forbidden fruit, he didn't sew together fig leaves and cover his nakedness out of some metaphysical sense of shame. It was because Eve took a look at him and laughed. That was the first laugh.

And ever since then the human condition has been a humorous condition.

As to prospects, I see a high probability of increasing cloudiness and a falling dollar. Any one of us could be struck down by a piece of space junk re-entering the atmosphere; or smushed by a small province flung by centrifugal force out of a disintegrating empire somewhere on the globe. But there's a probability bordering on certainty that, if you haven't been already, you'll be bitten by the laughing snake.

Jim Wayne Miller is a member of the Department of Modern Languages and Intercultural Studies at Western Kentucky University. He is the author of several volumes of poetry, and two novels, Newfound *and* His First Best Country. *He is in great demand as a speaker and leader of writing workshops. Dr. Miller is a graduate of Berea College and Vanderbilt University.*

Taking Laughter Seriously

Howard R. Pollio

The following is from a talk by Dr. Pollio at the Festival of Appalachian Humor at Berea College on July 17, 1993.

My subject is the psychology of humor, and I'll try to bring to you what anthropology, psychology, sociology, history, and literary studies tell us about humor. I'll also try to give you some insight into why those who are funny *are* funny. At the beginning, it's important to point out that there is a big difference between *being* funny and *knowing about* being funny, and many a scholar of humor has had some difficulty with this difference. Let's suppose as a scholar concerned with humor, that I am not funny, and suppose that I am trying to be funny but it doesn't work. What happens then is that you will shake your head and say, "I know why he studies humor; he's trying to find out what it is." That kind of attitude makes me wonder what people think about Dr. Ruth, or Dr. Kinsey or anyone else, who studies something that the audience is not sure that they are skillful at doing. It's different to know how to do something—and here I want you to know that I am talking about humor—and writing about it. What I try to do is to watch talented people and pick out things they do to see if I can find something general to say about it to you.

Before we start, however, I want you to think for a moment about Mardi Gras, or Eddie Murphy, or Richard Pryor, or about many of the comedians you may have seen on MTV. If you do, you'll become aware of something that perhaps wasn't obvious at first; humor many times is "R" rated, and occasionally "X" rated. I say this at the beginning because I once gave a talk on humor in which I didn't let the audience know that I knew that they knew that humor is "R" and "X" rated and deals with all sorts of taboo topics. What happened, when I didn't tell them, was that we became alienated from each other, and they didn't understand what I said, and they didn't like me. I don't like being unliked for a whole hour. So I tell you this: humor often deals with taboo topics.

What this means is that some of what I say will be "R" and "X" rated, but I want you to know that I don't enjoy talking about any of that. I don't enjoy it. I just hold it out there, as far away as possible, so we can examine it in a clinical sort of way. I'll do it in a scientific, dispassionate way, and it's not anything that's dear to me. So, just keep that in mind, I derive no pleasure from it. Steve Martin had a comedy show once called *Humor is Not a Pretty Thing.* Keep that in mind.

Now you ask, "How does a college professor become involved in the study of humor?" Well, the story goes like this. Some of you perform, and sometimes you have really great material. You feel, "I've got it this time. I'm going to be great. They're going to love it." Well, teachers feel like that too. I was teaching this class, and I wanted to teach the difference between denotation and connotation. Now *denotation* is what a thing is, like this microphone. *Connotation* is the emotional meaning a word has. For example, if I'm walking down the street and trip on something, what do I say? I use an explosive but expressive word that sounds something like "shoot." I've changed a vowel or two, but it won't fool anybody. Everybody knows what I meant to say. I'm not saying "shoot" to point anything out (denotation) on the ground; only to say how I feel (connotation)—as in the phrase "Aw shoot."

Okay, I was talking in class about the difference between denotation and connotation, and I thought, what examples can I give? Then I remembered this great record by George Carlin with a routine called "The Seven Words You Can Never Say on

Television." Now before class I'm thinking that this is going to be great. They are going to know that the words are not used literally—denotatively—but that they are used for expressive purposes—connotatively—and Carlin is always great. I'm sure it's really going to be funny, and I'm really ready to go into class. It's about the second day of class, and I bring in this big tape recorder, and I say, "I've invited a guest speaker today, and he's going to give a lecture on denotation and connotation, and by the way, do you all know the seven dirty words that you can't say on television? Well, I'm not going to tell you what they are, but I will tell you they are R-rated." So Carlin comes on and says the first word, which begins with "s." Actually, he was talking about all the things you can do with s____, and I was standing off to the side looking at my class. You know how undergraduates sit in class, eager, alert, brilliant, spending their father's and mother's money, so they sit up excited but relaxed. There were about three hundred of them out there, and when Carlin said the first word, suddenly I noticed the following happening. Everybody was closing up a little bit. Carlin went on to another word, and the audience kind of huddled down, crossed their arms and legs. Carlin talked a little more, and I saw the tops of three hundred heads. I had killed three hundred people. They closed up—legs closed, arms closed, heads down, nobody looking at me. I was thinking, "We've got trouble here." This is definitely not a class on denotation and connotation. So I said to the class, "What's happened here?"

One woman, a returning student, about thirty-five, said, "I don't know how to explain it to you, but I drew a picture that describes how I feel." So this is the picture she drew to express her experience.

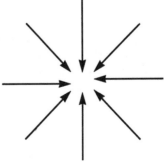

She said, "You can see by looking at these arrows that this is what I felt listening to the record. It's like there were all sorts of things pressing down on me; I guess what some people might call social forces."

Now I thought, "This is it! This is going to be a better class than anything that I could have brought in because it's coming from the class, and they're going to know what it means." So I said, "Social forces?" (This is how psychologists make a living. We repeat what the person says.) Then I got playful and said, "Let's take this arrow here at the bottom." She said, "Promise not to laugh?" (I never laugh.) She said, "That's my mother." "Your mother?" said I. "Yes, my mother." So I said, "Tell me more about that." (That's another thing we psychologists do—tell people to tell us more.) And she said, "That's my mother saying that nice girls don't laugh or respond to those words." "Tell me more about that," I said. She sort of squirmed and said, "If I know those words, my mother told me, then you know that I know the actions that go with the words, and if you know that I know the actions that go with the words, then you might ask me to perform those actions. So the best thing is to be embarrassed, to close up and not to acknowledge those things."

Now women know all of this, but men will probably say, "I didn't know that!" But, of course, they do know that. They've been to bars—when they were single, of course—and if they wanted to meet a young woman who was sitting at the bar, what did they do, what was their technique? The technique was to begin by saying something cute or funny, and what they were looking for was some sort of laugh or reaction from the young woman sitting there by them. So they start out with something cute, or something verbal, some clever language, and if the woman laughs, the man moves a little bit closer toward her. Then what does he do? He progressively gets more risque, and he knows something is possible when she laughs as the risque level of his humor goes up. It's a mating ritual among North Americans.

This is how I got interested in humor, right there in the classroom, and that student was absolutely correct. We talked about it, that somehow humor has something to do with what is important to people, but they don't know how to deal with it in any other way than by telling a joke about it. That's why humor is sometimes R-rated—because it deals with things that are really difficult to talk about in our culture, that we often don't know how to deal with in any other way. Keep the pointed arrows in mind as we talk further.

This, then, was the beginning of my research in humor, and it led to three questions. The first is what are the themes of humor—what sorts of things do people find funny? The second is how do you present these themes in order for them to be funny? And the third question is what do we know about the personal lives of people who are funny; that is, what do we know about comedians?

What are the themes of comedy? What is comedy about? How do you find out? I'm going to describe a study done in England that gathered about two hundred cartoons from *Punch* magazine, and then asked people to sort them into groups. When all the sorting was finished, they had four groups.

A cartoon that represents the first group is of a man sitting in his living room staring at his TV set, which is is floating in the air. In the caption the man says, "I think it is the vertical hold." There are two meanings involved here; the vertical hold used to adjust the picture and the much less common meaning of holding something and lifting it vertically, like a TV set. Given the cartoon, you can't really tell if this is sensible or not really sensible. So the first theme that humor is about is sense and nonsense. Sigmund Freud once said that the interesting thing about humor is that a lot of things that go on in humor are very much like what goes on in a dream. It has that same chaos that somehow makes sense but really doesn't make complete logical sense. This is the type of joke that everybody likes because it is a clean joke. There's nothing in this joke to bother anybody.

The philosopher who talked about this kind of humor was probably the least funny philosopher in the entire history of the world—Immanuel Kant. Kant explained humor as both sense and nonsense, or nonsense in sense. The type of humor this brings to mind is the pun. In a pun you have two meanings that get tied together that don't really make sense: Like, "What's the best way to drive a baby buggy?" (You tickle its feet.) It's a low level intellectual sort of thing, sense in nonsense.

The next group of cartoons is represented by one of a bunch of people standing around—some are hippies—and they are carrying signs. One fellow has a sign with no writing on it. The caption beneath the cartoon reads, "As far as I know he just hits people with it." This type of humor is called social satire and is a type of put-down directed against other people. If you think about your own experience in regard to this cartoon, you'll see that you probably feel superior to these people who are picketing, and to the poor guy who doesn't really have anything to picket about but who wants to picket anyway. Social satire of this kind puts someone or some idea down. This is a major theme: aggression against someone or something intending to put it down and thus make you feel superior. The philosopher who talked most about this kind of humor was the irascible English philosopher, Thomas Hobbes. As you may remember, it was he who defined human life as "nasty, brutish, and short." A fine fellow, that Tommy Hobbes.

Another cartoon deals with something related: It shows two English gentlemen standing in a formal garden looking at a hedge that has been clipped in the shape of a human hand with the middle finger erect in a well-known aggressive gesture. The caption reads, "I understand you fired the gardner." Actually, the original cartoon which appeared in *Punch* used the British form of the gesture, which involves two erect fingers—sort of in the shape of a "V." You will remember that in World War II, Winston Churchill would do a gesture with two fingers when he talked about the "Na-zees" (Nazis). "We shall have victory over the 'Na-zees,'" he would say, and combine it with this gesture. Churchill was a wonderful symbol monger, and he ended up being able to use the same gesture as both a "V" for victory for his team and to express aggression against the "Na-zees." There are many stories about Churchill and his ability to use symbols. By the way, when do you think the gardener got fired, before or after he did the hedge sculpture? It makes a difference. If he got fired beforehand, then it's the English gentleman who aggressed; if he did it afterward, it's the gardener who did the aggression. In either case, what you have is aggression, which defines the third major group of cartoons. And you have different levels of the social hierarchy, which also characterizes the third group. The cartoon pictures two English gentlemen and a gardener. They are of a different social status, so it is aggression against the higher social status by the lower social status, either in reprisal for being fired, or somewhat more gratuitously, as we might say. Although the third group of cartoons concerns aggression, it really is only a variant of the second theme; both groups, however, have to do with putting someone down and with making someone else—usually the reader—feel superior.

The fourth group of cartoons was defined by a picture of a naked man with his back to the reader, hands in the air, but with a barbell suspended by something in front of him between and about level with his hip joints! I can never decide whether this one is funnier to young men, old men, young women, or older women! As a young man I thought barbells were made of iron. Now, as an older man, I know they must be made of balsa wood. In any event, this cartoon presents the third major theme of humor: sex. A lot of comedy has some aspect of sexual humor in it.

Now, who do you think first wrote the theory that says that sex and aggression are behind most humor? That's right, Sigmund Freud. Freud's theory is basically that each of us is born with a lot of sexual and aggressive energy, and over the course of a lifetime, society tells us to cool it, to get a hold on it, maybe not to kill it but to kind of push it down or suppress it. But these sexual and aggressive urges percolate to the top. Think of a caldron bubbling with sexual and aggressive urges, and the lid of the pot comes up every now and then to let off some of the steam. That's roughly what Freud thought humor did—let off some of the steam to keep people from acting out in a sexual or aggressive way. Humor, in short, is a safety valve, a way to work off the stuff we can't work off, or can't deal with, in other ways.

So far, then, we have three major theories of humor: sense in nonsense (Kant), social satire and superiority (Hobbes), and sex (Freud). Now you are beginning to see why that drawing has so many arrows in it; each of those arrows represents a type of social force that we have to keep in check in some way, or else society couldn't function without great difficulty.

There is a fourth theory of humor that didn't come up in this study of *Punch* cartoons. In it's own way, it is perhaps the most serious of all the theories of humor, and this is the theory of the French philosopher Henri Bergson, who was interested in clowns. The question he based his theory on was: What's funny about clowns? He believed that they are funny because they fall! They shouldn't fall, but they do fall even when there is no obstacle. Bergson was interested in the contrast between human spontaneity—what he called the life force—and non-human objects, or what he called the mechanical aspect of life such as the physical body. Human beings tend to become mechanical and to repeat the same action and ideas over and over again. Bergson felt the need to correct human activity that becomes object-like, and the way to do this is to give people a moment of spontaneity. What humor is about, according to Bergson, is an attempt to provide us with an experience of spontaneity, an experience of unexpectedness, an experience of the life force flowing through us that is able to overcome the mechanical actions and the weary repetitiveness of unthinking everyday activity. The clown gives us a contrast between mechanical things that encrust us and the life forces that seek to jump out of the mechanical so as to express the human possibility for spontaneity and change and excitement.

Okay, there are four major themes we've discovered about humor: sense-nonsense, the put-down, sex, and spontaneity. The first of these is an intellectual theory, the second is a social theory, the third is a biological theory, and the fourth is a philosophical theory. As you can see, they all deal with some pretty important aspects of being human: Do things make sense? What position do I have in the social order? What can I do with my biological urges? And am I only a thing or is there something special about being a human?

The second question I promised to deal with concerns the way in which comic material is presented to an audience; more precisely, the different ways in which professional comedians do their comedy. As you know, some comedians do one-liners, a series of things that aren't all connected and slide from one thing to another leaving you kind of breathless. Henny Youngman exemplifies that approach. Comedians call this a *spritz,* which in German and Yiddish means "to spray." I want you to imagine diapering a baby; you take off the diaper, and *spritz!* Richard Pryor also does *spritz* routines some of the time.

The other way in which comedians present their material is in terms of a narrative. The story teller starts with a premise and develops the story. It may be loony as it can be, but it has a start, a middle, and an end—a punchline—and the whole thing makes nonsensical sense. It works. Bill Cosby is a narrative comedian. He tells stories which have this logically illogical structure.

To help us to understand how narrative and *spritz* routines affect the people listening to them, we need to remember the woman in my class who drew the arrows representing "social forces" and then ask where these social forces come from. Basically, her "social forces" came from people around her as well as from other people she was imagining. If we generalize her experience, people tend to worry about whom they are sitting with if a comedian talks trash and does it in a *spritz* format. People also tend to wonder what kind of person the comedian is. Think about reactions to Richard Pryor. You wonder where did he grow up? How did he get like this? Why does he talk like this?

In contrast, you react differently to the narrative, or story-telling, comedian. He sets a story in motion, then gets the audience to start thinking about similar situations or to identi-fy with the people in the story. A storyteller takes you into a nonsensical world that is *not here,* and *not now.* It's a magic world created by the storyteller's art. The *spritz* comedian, on the other hand, forces you into the immediacy of your present situation, so you say, who is this guy and who am I with in this situation? What seems to have happened in my class is that Carlin was doing a *spritz* routine that forced the students to worry about who they were with and how they would be seen by the people they were with. Remember, *spritz* is here-and-now; storytelling is there-and-then, and they direct us to differ-ent experiences.

Another question I promised to answer is what do we know about comedians? The first thing about professional comedians we know is that they are really smart, and that they love lan-guage. They really love the sound of language and the multiple meanings words have. When a sample of about fifty male New York comedians were given a set of I.Q. tests, the average was 138! That is very, very good! The second thing that is important to know about comedians is that they are older, by and large, than most other performers. It takes a while to learn the craft, and you need to learn it in front of an audience. You can't learn it practicing in front of a mirror, like a dancer might, or in an empty studio. You need a live audience.

Another interesting thing about comedians has to do with the Rohrshach ink blot tests. Think of what it would be like to give ink blot tests to Bill Cosby, or to Don Rickles! Comedians tend to see a little bit of deception in everything; what this means is that they see a lot of masks and "nice monsters" in the ink blots. They see little things and tend to be very sensitive to tiny spots on the cards. They also tend to project into the blots angels and devils that only they see. And they see things falling down. If you think about these four things: nice monsters, teeny objects, angels and devils, and things that fall down, you can see each of the major humor theories at work: things aren't what they seem (sense in nonsense—Kant); small-not-important objects become important (inferiority-superiority—Hobbes); angels and devils (taboo items—Freud); and things that fall down when they shouldn't (clowns—Bergson). What this means is that comedians saw in ink blots the themes of humor and the stuff of which comedy is made. In short, they are uniquely sensitive to what humor is all about even when looking at ambiguous cards.

Now, we have to do the hard part, tying all these ideas together. Let's start by going back again to the drawing of the arrows pointing in. This is the way I tend to think about humor. We are always surrounded by, and confined by, social forces, and these social forces cause us to worry about such issues as what's sensible, who's more (or less) important than I, what should I do with the taboo feelings I have, and will I fall down and never get up? So the question we have to face every day for life is: What do we do with these social forces that tell us how to behave and to think about these issues? To help us understand, let's look at another drawing.

In this drawing, the arrows are all pointing out, not in. What this is meant to suggest is that periodically we need to (and actually do) explode the whole range of social forces that tell us how we should feel about what words mean, social position, taboo feelings and even life and death. How? If I told you this 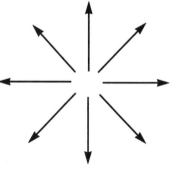 drawing was meant to symbolize a laugh you would have little difficulty in seeing it that way. What a laugh is, then, is an explosion from the terrible and awful restraints that society puts on us to experience things the way it wants us to experience them.

That's why we *love* to laugh. It's an exhilarating moment of absolute non-confinement by any of the various social forces. In the moment that we laugh, we are radically free from all the cares and all the concerns, all the *oughts* and all the *shoulds*, that are in our lives and that are necessary for there to be any society at all.

But I have to say one more thing about a laugh, and it's perhaps the saddest thing that I have to say. Think about what happens if you laugh too long, without stop. What happens is, your face start hurting, your sides start hurting, and you can't breathe. What does this say? To me it says that while a laugh may provide the exhilarating experience of breaking free of all of the social constraints and oughts that confine us—our body, other people, our morality—we cannot stay in a situation of no morality, no body, no social constraint for *too* long. God has put into us the need to be mindful of our body, our social situation, and our morality. What laughter does for us—what humor does through laughter—is to provide us with exhilarating moments in which, for a time, and a short time it is, we break free of all those cares, oughts, and responsibilities that have been laid on us since we were children. Laughter is the radical gesture of freedom from constraint which, at the same time, recognizes that ultimately we cannot be without constraints or rules. This then is the human condition: to experience the exhilaration of freedom through laughter which then ultimately forces us to reaffirm the need for social order and constraint.

We can no more stay forever in a laugh than we can exist independent of social forces—forces that simultaneously limit and support us—and it is this complex set of relationships that humor forces us to confront on each and every occasion that we laugh.

Howard R. Pollio, a native of New York City, holds a doctorate in psychology from the University of Michigan. He is Distinguished Service Professor, Department of of Psychology, and Senior Research Fellow, Learning Research Center, the University of Tennessee, Knoxville.

Other Books from August House Publishers

LAUGHTER IN APPALACHIA
Loyal Jones and Billy Edd Wheeler
Paperback $8.95 / ISBN 0-87483-032-X

CURING THE CROSS-EYED MULE
Loyal Jones and Billy Edd Wheeler
Paperback $9.95 / ISBN 0-87483-083-4

HOMETOWN HUMOR, U.S.A
Loyal Jones and Billy Edd Wheeler
Hardback $19.95 / ISBN 0-87483-343-4
Paperback $9.95 / ISBN 0-87483-342-6

THE PREACHER JOKE BOOK
Loyal Jones
Paperback $6.95 / ISBN 0-87483-087-7

OUTHOUSE HUMOR
Billy Edd Wheeler
Paperback $5.95 / ISBN 0-87483-065-6

ROPING CAN BE HAZARDOUS TO YOUR HEALTH
Southwestern Humor by Curt Brummet
Paperback $6.95 / ISBN 0-87483-146-6

OZARK MOUNTAIN HUMOR
Edited by W.K. McNeil
Hardback $18.95 / ISBN 0-87483-085-0
Paperback $8.95 / ISBN 0-87483-086-9

A FIELD GUIDE TO SOUTHERN SPEECH
Charles Nicholson
Hardback $6.95 / ISBN 0-87483-098-2

AUGUST HOUSE PUBLISHERS, INC.
P.O. BOX 3223
LITTLE ROCK, AR 72203
1-800-284-8784